A COW IN THE HOUSE

And Nine Other Stories

A COW IN THE HOUSE

And Nine Other Stories

by

BENEDICT KIELY

LONDON
VICTOR GOLLANCZ LTD
1978

© Benedict Kiely 1978

ISBN 0 575 02519 0

MADE AND PRINTED IN GREAT BRITAIN BY
THE GARDEN CITY PRESS LIMITED
LETCHWORTH, HERTFORDSHIRE
SG6 1JS

DEDICATION

For Anne Kiely
in Geneva.

ACKNOWLEDGMENTS

'There Are Meadows In Lanark', 'Bluebell Meadow', 'The Night We Rode With Sarsfield', 'Elm Valley Valerie' first appeared in *The New Yorker*, 'My Contemplations Are Of Time . . .' in *The Irish Press*, 'A Cow In The House' in *The Texas Quarterly*, and 'The Fairy Women of Lisbellaw' in *The Journal of Irish Literature*, University of Delaware.

The verses by W. B. Yeats quoted on pages 16 and 19 are from 'The Lamentation of the Old Pensioner', reprinted by permission of M. B. Yeats and The Macmillan Co. of London and Basingstoke, from *The Collected Poems of W. B. Yeats*.

CONTENTS

"MY CONTEMPLATIONS ARE OF TIME . . ."

T HERE'S A MAN I know who went to school with me who owns a public-house. He spent ten years in Chicago, but that's irrelevant. Once when I congratulated him on the peace of the village he lives in he said: I've merited that peace, I spent ten years in Chicago.

That was nine years ago, the last time I was in the village.

He's not the only man who went to school with me who's fortunate enough to own a pub but this pub has one remarkable thing about it: its backroom is as full of clocks as old-fashioned jeweller-watchmaker-clockmaker shops used to be long ago in rural places and provincial towns. Except that the clocks are not ticking, nor chiming, in case the backroom boys might think the man of the house too damned insistent on that business of Time gentlemen, please.

The reason for this proliferation of clocks is simply that my friend's brother, who lives in the same village but never saw Chicago, is a clock-collector and the collection has overflowed. Nobody any longer passes any remark about the clocks: they are part of the furniture like books and pictures in a rich man's house. Since they all point to different times they thereby make a mockery of time.

The Ulster village in which the clocks have overflowed from one house to another is quiet and beautiful: at one end a bridge under which a small stream flows down to Lough Erne; at the other end, and looking down the street, a Protestant church, grey stone, a slender steeple, eighteenth or early nineteenth century. The surrounding Ulster countryside is a filigree pattern of blue lake and deep water-meadow, so intricate that it must always be a torment to the cartographer who, to represent it exactly, would need the special talents of the holy men who in the middle ages made the illuminated manuscripts and—according to the poet Austin Clarke—had a hand in heaven.

To the west this green-and-blue pattern is hooked on to the lonely Cuilcha mountains where the River Shannon comes mysteriously from a deep silent pool in the middle of a meadow. From the narrow roads, smothered in deep hedges, signposts point to fishing-stands and boating-slips and little harbours with musical names.

Recently my old alarm clock which had sounded reveille for me for many years, here in Ireland and in several States of the Union, gave up the ghost, dying silently in the night: I purchased him in Eugene, Oregon. As I did the right shoe that I wear around the house, the survivor to a pair, the left being the survivor of another pair bought in Atlanta, Georgia. So that standing here in Donnybrook, Dublin, which is now a select semi-suburb but where there used to be a famous fighting fair, I bestride a lot of the United States: one foot by Stone Mountain and the sands of the Chattahoochie, the other beyond the Cascades.

That alarm clock had been a good friend, his shrill clarion had become music to my ears. With regret I interred him and bought another, blackfaced with yellow hands and numerals, who lasted for exactly a week when an accidental tumble, and not a severe one, put an end also to his ticking and alarming. No amount of shaking and persuading could get him back to work and with something like fury I delivered him one evening to a plastic trashbag and bought yet another.

Then on a Thursday morning, when the lorries of the Cleansing Department of Dublin Corporation come my way, I walk to a shed in my back-garden to carry the trash-bags to my front gate. In the mildest January in what they call living memory the green sprouts of the daffodils are high above the ground. Across the road in Herbert Park, the daisies are displayed in hundreds. John Berryman said that Herbert Park was the most beautiful park since Bombay. Did he mean that Bombay was so beautiful or that there is also a beautiful park in Bombay?

In the half-dead pear tree at the bottom of my garden two magpies are mocking a foolish young cat, dancing when it pleases them from branch to branch, dodging him with well-tailored ease, screaming shrill evil laughter to each other. Paying no attention to cat or magpies the two doves from the convent grounds over thataway are pecking fastidiously at my tray of breadcrumbs. Those doves get so much to eat around the convent that at times they have difficulty in taking off, looking somewhat like those transport planes that have big heads on them—like the rabbits when they had the myxomatosis. But although slow-moving the doves are quite fierce and the cats leave them alone.

Squadrons of sparrows come and go through a bride-blossom bush, a bird-delighting tree, that even when leafless draws them in hundreds: I have two blackbirds and a missel-thrush and once, for God's sake, had a green linnet, right, you might say, in the heart of the city or, at any rate, half an hour's walk from Stephen's Green.

The townward morning traffic is as heavy on Morehampton Road as it was on Ponce de Leon in Atlanta.

In the house I live in two British officers, secret service men, were shot dead, and one wounded trying to get out through what is now my bedroom window into this garden where the magpies mock the cat. That was in 1920, at the order of Michael Collins, on one of Ireland's many bloody Sundays. Later on in the day the crown forces invaded Croke Park, a crowded Gaelic stadium in the north city, and shot at everything in sight: reprisals and reprisals and reprisals creeps in this petty pace from day to day, and all our yesterdays, etc.

Carrying two black plastic bags through the house I am when I hear the ticking: an alarming sound in Ireland these days, and no pun intended. It could be the deathwatch beetle or the telltale heart, it could be something more modern or much worse—and I am about to drop the bags and ring the army when I remember the clock. With messing and difficulty I exhume him. From, as you might expect, the absolute bottom of the bag. And there he is now, buried alive and resurrected, with an impertinent black face, ticking away as cheery as a grasshopper and even keeping excellent time.

A while in the trash-bag may be the true way to cure recalcitrant clocks and other people: and now I have two men to wake me in the morning which is a bit of a joke since—and possibly because of a guilty conscience or that my father was in the British army—I am automatically an early riser if I haven't been out too late the night before.

This resurrected clock may be some sort of relation to the alarm clock that my Aunt Rose, who was also my godmother, brought back from Philadelphia with her sometime in the 1930s. Alarm clocks were not then all that plentiful in rural places and provincial towns, people depended more on roosters, hungry babies, church bells or the rising sun. So that when that American clock stopped working it was considered worth while to bring him to a famous jeweller and watchmaker who was also, like my aunt, a returned American—and a most remarkable man.

For one thing it was rumoured that he had very grave doubts as to whether God existed. Or if God did exist then the jeweller had even graver doubts about the quality of his personality.

He was a tall man, six feet six, dressed in good dark cloth and a cap with a button on the top of it, carried an army officer's cane with silver top and steel ferrule, went walking in the evenings or Sunday afternoons with three Irish setters, happy, shining, well-fed, well-groomed, active animals. One day a young lady who sang in the church choir—her Adeste is still in my ears—called in to him to collect a clock that he had repaired. She was on the way to the choir. He said: You are off now to that man's house to sing.

She said—joking: I am. Won't you come with me?

He thought it over for a while: No, I could not bring myself to enter a man's house who, if I offended him, would treat me worse than I'd treat my dogs.

But he smiled as he said it because he was, also, towards his fellow-mortals, a man of infinite affability who had seen the world and could talk about it, and when the two ladies, my mother and my aunt, brought in the clock, he and my aunt talked for an hour about the woods of Maine, the villages of New England, about what the forsythia and dogwood would be like in the South at that time of the year—it was that time of the year—about Niagara Falls and the plains of the Midwest and so on. Then at last he put his jeweller's spyglass into his eye and studied the innards of the clock, and shook his head sadly and said: Beyond human aid. Even the Almighty, in whom I'm sure you good ladies believe, could do nothing with this one.

He handed it to my mother who, taken unawares, dropped it on the floor where it began to alarm like the fire brigade, and not only to alarm but to go: for when the alarm ceased, the loud double-tick could be heard competing with the ticks of all the other clocks in the shop.

He picked it up with great good humour and handed it, this time to my aunt. He said: You may tell the parish priest that the Lord has judged me and found me wanting.

For whatever reason, that clock ran for another ten years until the god of all clocks, or the King of the Great Clock Tower, who may have a face like a clock, called his subject to himself.

The only other well-known atheist in our town was a postman or mail-carrier who was also on the reserve of the Royal Air Force. He was a small man who talked and gestured a lot, recited at parties, in imitation of Bransby Williams, about the green eye of the little yellow god and about dead men's bones where the wild wind moans on the lonely Yukon trail; had a colossal collection of recordings of classical music, and a face dyed a sort of purple-brick colour from carrying the mail in all weathers into valleys in the Sperrin mountains where the great Hugh O'Neill had once trained his swordsmen to meet the soldiers of the first Elizabeth of England.

Recalled to the colours a little after Munich the postman was involved in that business around Ostend and Dunkirk, and afterwards, heading for Cherbourg in a hurry, he met a girl in the back of a truck: a careful girl whose peasant origins were in the

Auvergne. He married her though not, I suppose, in the back of the truck, and brought her home with him, and her canny housekeeping staggered the natives. Her sister-in-law, who was pious and gentle and married to a barber, told my mother that after the Frenchwoman sliced a loaf she locked up the crumbs.

But the postman and herself and the classical recordings lived happily together and she learned to speak English the way we did, and although his recent European experiences had, if anything, hardened his theological or untheological opinions, she did occasionally persuade him, for the sake of appearances and sociability, to go to Mass. The tall jeweller and clockmaker who walked the red setters and treated them decent was a sociable man, but he had no such weakness before human, or divine, respects.

St Exupery, flying to Arras on a mission of war, looked down on the shining spring day, the ripening fruit, the rising wheat, the chicks filling plumply in the barnyard: and also knew that death was at his elbow. He saw no reason why the peace of a spring day should constitute a contradiction to the idea of death: Why should the sweetness of life be a matter for irony?

But as he flew and looked down he knew that the spring had broken down and the season was out of order.

He had flown over abandoned threshing-machines and binders, motor-cars deserted in ditches, a village square under water while the village faucet or fountain or pump "stood open and the stream flowed on". He thought, ridiculously he said, of clocks out of order: All the clocks of France—out of order. Clocks in their church steeples. Clocks on railway stations. Chimney clocks in empty houses. A charnel-house of clocks. He said to himself that: The war is a thing in which clocks are no longer wound up. In which beets are no longer gathered in. In which farmcarts are no longer greased. And that water, collected and piped to quench men's thirst and to whiten the Sunday laces of the village women—that water stands now in a pool, flooding the square before the village church.

*   *   *

There was another clockmaker in that street, not a tall, talkative, returned American, but a tiny Irishman who had never been further from home than an excursion to Bundoran by the Donegal sea could take him. What his religious beliefs were I can't say but I have a feeling that men who continually contemplate time may easily incline to scepticism.

He came into my imagination the day we had broken the watch that Shorty Simpson's father had given him for Christmas, not broken it deliberately but by accident and in a wrestling match. It was an Ingersoll watch with a black face and phosphorescent digits, and a phosphorescent railway engine puffing across the centre of the black face. It was a valuable watch, worth all of 30 old pence. Shorty's father was an engine driver and that may have had something to do with the choice of décor. In this wrestling match we were pretending to be Fionn MacCumhail—that was Lanty Cassidy who was a born leader—and his Fenian warriors in ancient Ireland. Lanty fell on top of Shorty who leaped up with a roar when he heard the crunch and groped in frenzy for a patch watch-pocket that a fond mother had stitched on to the front of his trousers. Then he sat down on the ground and began to cry. Then he stood up and raised a hullabaloo and swore he would tell his father and mother and all the adults from Antrim to Aughrim.

It was poor behaviour for a follower of the heroic Fionn, but we felt too deeply for him, and for the nature of the disaster, to utter a word of reproof. Nobody else owned a watch. Shorty was a spoiled child.

We sat in council in a circle around the big tree on the top of Gallows Hill, as the men of Fionn, according to the story-books, might after a hunt or a foray have sat on the Hill of Allen in the County Kildare. The big tree was only the stump of a tree. But somebody with nothing better to do, or perhaps to make a tethering base for cattle or goats, had once driven deep into the trunk two iron bars with hooked ends. That was enough to make us think that people had been hanged from that tree, thus giving the hill its grisly name and the area around the tree stump a special awe.

We studied the damage to the watch. The glass was gone. The hands were paralysed. The back was dented and wouldn't open so that it was no longer possible to see what, if anything, was going on in the very soul of the machine. The railway engine which gleamed so splendidly by night was a sad sight in the daylight of ruin. It puffed on, going nowhere forever.

Shorty gulped and tried to be brave. He was a close-cropped blond short-sighted little boy with a squint and thick silver-rimmed spectacles.

—There's nothing for it, said Fionn MacCumhail, but Jamie the little jeweller. They say he can bring the dead back to life.

—That means, somebody said, going all the way down to John Street.

—The police are down there, said yet another Fenian.

—They're after the whip-fighters still.

—They're only after Tall John.

—They're after the jing-bang lot of us.

—It's a big risk to take.

These whip-fights had taken place between the boys of the Hill and the boys of Brook Street, another lively quarter at the far end of the town. Nobody paid much attention to them until Tall John, a muscular dwarf of a Hill boy with a curious sense of humour, tied a cut-throat razor to the end of a horse-whip and drove both armies before him from Gallows Hill to John Street. Two shop windows were broken and one old lady knocked down, and the police appealed to. No arrests were made but terror descended on Brook Street and the Hill, and whips were confiscated, or hidden, as in old days of rebellion steel pikes were hidden in cornstacks in haggards or in the thatched roofs of mountain cabins:

> Though lads are making pikes again
> For some conspiracy,
> And crazy rascals rage their fill
> At human tyranny,
> My contemplations are of Time
> That has transfigured me.

That was what the lamenting old pensioner said in the poem by William Butler Yeats. What Lanty Cassidy said the day he broke the watch was that if we were all feared to go into town with him he would go himself: Hand me the watch, Shorty.

We couldn't let our captain shame us so we went down after him from the Hill, crossed the Fair Green or Cow Commons, clattered in nailed boots along the blue-flagged sidewalk of John Street, shops and offices all around us, passed the Methodist meeting-house where the air was always fluttering with pigeons, and came to the little jeweller's where John MacBride who was musical said he could stand all day listening to the ticking and the chiming.

—So many clocks, he said, of all shapes, sizes and sounds, in one small room.

Carrying the watch in his cupped hands Lanty entered. The rest of us in holy awe looked through the window at the dumb-show going on inside. Jimmy was a grizzled gentle stump of a man and, by relativity, the jeweller's glass stuck in his left eye looked like a miniature telescope. He had a sad saintly little smile. Expertly he opened the watch, as we had been unable to do, switched on a light that was under a green shade on the counter, applied the light and the eye-telescope to the watch. He shook his head sadly, handed the watch back to Lanty, and with the cry of a soul in distress Shorty was in through the door to gather to himself his beloved machine. We followed like chief mourners.

—Not Tompion himself, said Jamie, and he was the greatest clockmaker who ever lived, could make that engine move again.

He may not have said exactly that, but recently I read a book about Tompion—and it seems an apt reference.

He groped under the counter, came up with a silvery pocket-watch, shook it, set it, wound it, held it to his ear and nodded with satisfaction.

—How about a swop young Simpson, he said. Your watch for one that goes. I might get a spare part or two out of yours. Here, take this one.

He handed it out towards Shorty who backed away suspiciously.

—Can you see it in the dark?

—Well, no. But you could always strike a light.

—It's no good, said Shorty, if you can't see it in the dark. And there's no railway engine on it.

—No. But the works work.

—It's not a fair swop.

Then the little man said: I tell you what, take the two of them. That way at night you can look at one and listen to the other.

Solomon himself could not have made a better judgement, yet to this day I feel that Shorty was not satisfied and never forgave us, and now as I listen to my two alarm clocks galloping away together I remember the day we tiptoed into that shadowy, ticking, chiming sanctuary and listened to the wisdom of Jamie and the many voices of time.

Deposed and in his prison cell the sad Shakesperean king lamented that he had wasted time and now did time waste him:
. . .

For now hath time made me his numbering clock;
My thoughts are minutes; and with sighs they jar
Their watches to mine eyes, the outward watch,
Whereto my finger, like a dial's point,
Is pointing still, in cleansing them from tears.
Now, sir, the sound that tells what hour it is,
Are clamorous groans, which strike upon my heart,
Which is the bell: so sighs and tears and groans
Show minutes, times and hours—but my time
Runs posting on in Bolingbroke's proud joy,
While I stand fooling here, his Jack o' th' clock.

In that peaceful Ulster lake-and-meadowland where nine years ago I saw how the clocks had overflowed and kept no time, a man, in the summer of last year, disappeared on the way from his work to his home—a distance of three miles. He was a county councillor. He was missing from July into mid-August when an early morning fisherman on one of the little lakes that go to make up the filigree pattern of blue and green found the body, badly decomposed and with a 56-pound weight attached, floating close to the shore.

The man had died from a gunshot wound. His burned-out car, once a white Mazda, was found five miles away. When he failed to come home from work at his usual time his wife—that part of the world being the way it now is—raised the alarm. Bloodstains and shirt-buttons were found in the laneway leading to his house. One report said that a neighbour that evening had heard five shots. The murdered man was 33 years of age like Christ himself, but, unlike Christ, he had four small children. Each of the groups of gunmen now murdering in those parts blamed the other for the murder but up to this moment no culprit has been found.

Meanwhile the lakes and little harbours and the fishing-stands and the grass-meadows are as quiet and lovely as ever, but it is possible that one lake, for some people, will never be the same again: and the clocks in the backroom, as far as I know, still make no sound.

Oh time is a fine thing if you can catch it and keep a firm hold on it.

You'll remember how, in the Yeats poem I mentioned, the old pensioner sits out of the rain under a broken tree and remembers how once, in good company, his chair was nearest to the fire when people talked of love or politics. He looks at the rain and thinks of the women of his youth:

> There's not a woman turns her face
> Upon a broken tree,
> But yet the beauties that I loved
> Are in my memory;
> I spit into the face of Time
> That has transfigured me.

MAKE STRAIGHT FOR THE SHORE

BREAKFAST WAS perfunctory and the main meal of the day was taken at a place called the Continental Café or the Café Continental where we used to eat bangers and mash by the hundredweight and dance with the waitresses to a voice and a tune on the radio: There's a lovely lake in London where Rhododendrons grow.

It was a very popular tune at the time. I can't remember if that other song had then surfaced: At the Café Continental like a fool I fell in love.

Not one of the three of us did fall in love there. The waitresses were all as fat as fools: from snapping-up all day long unconsidered trifles of bangers and mash. Our ideal then was Ginger Rogers, the young Ginger Rogers, the Ginger Rogers of *Roxy Hart*: her dancing was different.

When there wasn't a lovely lake in London there were red sails in the sunset, way out on the sea. We picked up a lot of our current and popular music by hanging around bicycle shops: We'll build a nest way up in the west 'neath a sky of heavenly blue, a one-room flat and a two-pants suit and three square meals a day, I've told every little star just how sweet I think you are, with a carpet on the floor made of buttercups and clover. In more elevated moments we listened to John McCormack and Enrico Caruso and had strong controversy as to which of them was the greater. Caruso had, hadn't he, broken a wine-glass just by singing into it? But McCormack was one of our own.

Radio sets were scarce, so were the fourpences for the pit in the picture-house and scarcer still was the money to buy the records we coveted and not every household had a gramophone. So bicycle shops it had to be. We never even wondered: why bicycle shops? Why not confectioneries or groceries or newsagencies, where you

might expect music to go with literature: or draperies or haber-
dasheries or hardware merchants?

Busto looked like this: I draw a circle supported by a larger circle
supported by two stumpy rectangles. Lanko looked like this: I
draw a small circle supported on two parallel lines. They were both
Christian Brothers and both surnamed Burke, one from Dublin
and the other from Tipperary, and because of them the three of us
were in Belfast City dancing with the waitresses, walking the town
like men of the town, watching the dark clouds of starlings around
the gigantic but dignified Victorian city hall and in our leisure
moments doing an entrance examination for the British civil service. In the late spring the clouds of starlings are a sight to see.

This day Lanko came to me after Latin class and said: Because
of that arithmetic paper you haven't a hope in this world or the
next of getting King's scholarship.

He was, as you may have guessed, a tall man, so tall he looked
thin which he really wasn't, and he had a handsome blackavised
face, a gentle musical Munster accent, and all the matrons in the
town and a lot of the maidens were mad about him—the inaccess-
ible, almost, in those days. He had played hurling for Tipperary,
and the long black Christian Brothers' habit, especially long in his
case, went very well with the easy athletic way he walked.

—No the arithmetic paper, he said, would be your Waterloo.

It was my final year in secondary school in an Ulster provincial
town and, at that time and in those parts, the only future for the
average secondary student was to go to training college for two
years and resurface as a primary-school teacher so as to teach
primary students to become secondary students. You could, if you
were lucky, become an artisan, or dig holes in the street for the
town council and nobody would ever see anything of you except
the top of your head. As in greater towns like New York somebody
was always digging holes in the street: constant employment. You
could, of course, become a priest or a nun or, if your parents had
the means, you could go to the university and follow one of the
professions, or become a secondary teacher and teach other

secondary students to become primary teachers, and so on. The United States produces every year, somebody told me, 30,000 doctors of philosophy and there can't be that many philosophers in the whole world: take a look at it, for God's sake.

But in 1936 about 50 per cent of my class were doomed to sit for this examination called King's scholarship and to go, if they were successful, to a place in Twickenham, near London, called Strawberry Hill, sacred to the memory of Horace Walpole who had lived there and of Seán Ó Faoláin who had taught there, and to become primary-school teachers. The big hurdle in that examination was an arithmetic paper of four diabolical problems, and the way to take it was: if question one didn't provide an answer, to take a run at two and three and four so that, with the law of averages and good luck and one of them out of the way, there were fewer to bewilder you and your confidence was quadrupled. Or is quadrupled, I wonder, exactly what I mean?

A good friend of mine wouldn't or couldn't work that way: he'd stick with question one until the bell rang, with the result that he never became a primary-school teacher. Instead he became a wealthy businessman and still is one, and a credit to the country and a great benefit, I'm told, to the poor in the town he lives in.

As for myself, I never even attempted or was allowed to attempt King's scholarship. The thought of that arithmetic paper turned me off, and subtraction was the only sort of arithmetic I was ever any good at, and Lanko said gently: No, dear boy, you'd never take that hurdle. But there is this exam for the British civil service if you don't mind serving the king, and it's becoming very popular nowadays, good conditions, good pay, you can rise to the top, no sectarianism across the water, and you could see a bit of the world into the bargain, beginning with Belfast where the exam is held.

Busto didn't put it so gently: Busto had a kind heart but blunter ways, picked up, perhaps, in the scrum when in his youth he had played rugby football for Blackrock; and about the kind heart I didn't find out until years later I met him in Dublin when he was ailing in health and wasn't even Busto any more, and his cheeks were hollow and his feet flat and his clothes had grown too big for him. But Busto he still assuredly was when he stopped me one day in the corridor outside the chemistry lab. and told me of my prospects in the service of the King of England. He (Busto) had a deft way of lifting youths by their incipient sidelocks and occasionally booting them in the buttocks in a friendly but efficient fashion. For Blackrock, it was said, he had been the supremo among place-kickers.

He was the Brother Superior and students were sent to him for punishment, and they got it. One poor sniveller came in from a history class to meet his deserts and his whipping. So Busto says: What are you here for?

—Please sir, I forgot how a man died.

—Why, says Busto, didn't you say he forgot to draw his breath.

And lifted the non-historian with one well-placed boot.

But at the door of the stinks lab. he merely tweaked my nose and said jovially: You can't put two and two together. You'll never get King's scholarship. You'll never be able to put two and two together. But there's the British civil service. To judge by the stupid things they do in Whitehall they'll never notice you in the crowd. Proceed and prosper and God save the king.

Unkicked, I proceeded.

And there we were, the chosen three, living on bangers and mash and dancing with fat waitresses to the tunes of a lovely lake in London and swift wings we must borrow, make straight for the shore, and more besides. As I said, we knew the tunes already from our regular scholarly attendance at a bicycle shop, one very special bicycle shop: and for the moment we were gentlemen on the town, three fine free right feet and fellows for them, truly at large and out of the reservation for the first time in our lives, living in an hotel at the back of the city hall and studying the black driving clouds of shrieking starlings. Have the bombs, I wonder, dispersed the starlings?

For the last time I was in that hotel the screaming birds were still blackening the sky but the bombs were just beginning. Thick as night or locusts the starlings were around the city hall and in the hotel there was no water in the taps. The hotel has changed its name now, or it may not, because of the bombs, be there any more; one new and neighbouring hotel was bombed nineteen times, room service how are you. But eight years ago it was still there and had then changed its name, and I sat sipping in the lounge, looking at a pop-group called the Necromancers and remembering the bright blonde hair of Trudi. Looking at, not listening to, I'm overjoyed to say, for the Necromancers were merely relaxing after their labours of the night before. A few of them were asleep or half asleep. There was little talk between them. They were possibly saving their breath for the night to come. An interestingly-mixed group: West Indian, Afro-American, European, which I could see for myself, Irish and English and German which I had been told. Two of them who were not slumbering ordered drinks, real drinks, which surprised me: who had always assumed that pop-groups and show-bands lived on cow's milk and pills. A slim young blonde girl from the hotel staff brought them a telegram. O the blonde head of my Trudi long ago when Rhododendrons grew around the lovely lake in London. As she bent to deliver the telegram the girl blushed to the backs of her mini-skirtless thighs at having been chosen for the honour of carrying a message that came through the air, to the corner where the gods reposed: no harpers those to learn their songs and melodies in bicycle shops, red sails in the sunset I'm trusting in you.

Later as I sat at dinner with a BBC ballad-singer and a Dublin political, both convivial men, we heard a great sound. At first we thought that a large part of Belfast had been blown up. But later still it was reported that a meteorite had splashed down, hitting nobody as far as was known—the heavens were harmless—in a peat-bog in County Down.

The ballad-singer said: At all times of crisis and calamity there are signs in the sky.

The political said: Rockets from Russia.

The hotel was full of pressmen. Rumour, painted all over with tongues, was running wild to tell us that, for instance, the papishes were to march on Sandy Row at ten o'clock when the pubs closed.

To prove what?

Why, to prove to the Protestant Sandy Rowers that the IRA did not blow up the aqueduct near the big reservoir in the Silent Valley in the Mountains of Mourne: which was why there was no water in the taps in the hotel nor in the hospitals nor anywhere else, almost, in Belfast.

That demonstration would have made a lot of sense: just as much as when the Holy Rollers of Dayton, Tennessee, proved to their own satisfaction, by rolling all together on the ground, that man was not descended from the monkey.

Trudi I could see quite plainly, although the dining-room, which we three students long ago hadn't much frequented, had been altered and redecorated and, anyway, her sort of hotel-work didn't bring her into the dining-room.

Later still we heard that the rumour was false and that the demonstration was not to take place. But the pressmen who, because of the unhappy nature of their calling, are obliged to give at least a friendly nod to every rumour, were already on the way to Sandy Row, just to see.

We had an excellent dinner and much wine. Later still we heard that the meteorite had splashed down not in County Down but in County Derry: and jocose speculation continued about the nature of the great sound.

The Holy Ghost descending at long last on the collapsing parliament in Stormont Castle.

Dr Ian Paisley ascending from the Crumlin Road Jail in a flaming flying saucer and all the trumpets sounding for him from the other side as they did for Mr Standfast. For Dr Paisley was that night in Pauline chains for disturbing the peace outside the Presbyterian assembly building five minutes walk away in Fisherwick Place: in which pinnacled, dark-stone, ice-cold building Bill and Fuzzy-Wuzzy and myself had long before sat, more or less, for that civil service examination.

The evening papers had reported that Dr Paisley's aide-de-camp, the Rev. Mr Foster, who had just been released, said that Dr Paisley was the happiest man in the prison, happier even than the governor, because Dr Paisley was with God.

The ballad-singer wondered if governors of prisons were necessarily happy.

The political wondered if governors of prisons were of necessity not with God.

We sipped our brandy and I remembered Trudi.

Later still I tried to tell the manager, a brusque, busy fellow, how a female member of the staff of that hotel had, away before his time, kept me out of the second world war and thus may, by several years, have postponed the German defeat. But he seemed in too much of a hurry to try or to bother to understand.

There she was on the very first morning the three of us woke up in that hotel. We had a room each, small rooms and not over-elegant but independent and our own. Belfast we had often visited, on the lead with parents or led by teachers, to rugby games in Ravenhill, but this was different. What could a man have done or said to Trudi if he had been sandwiched between parents or crocodiled on the sporting road to Ravenhill? O, the long bright blonde hair of Trudi, an Easter sun dancing over a new-arisen world. In the hometown I knew two sisters, one called Deborah, the other Rachel, Presbyterians, naturally, with names like that, but never a girl called Trudi and never a girl so blonde.

—Trudi, I said, is your name really and truly Trudi.

—That's what my father and mother call me, and my brothers and sisters all seven of them, and the neighbours, who speak to me. Where I come from everybody doesn't speak to everybody.

She was a wit. She had to be, she was so beautiful.

—Do you come from Germany? Or Switzerland?

Switzerland was all hotels and mountains.

Her accent should have told me but I hadn't travelled much at the time and all beautiful women spoke with the same accent. She was, at that moment, stripping my bed preparatory to re-making it: the lass that made the bed to me, I knew my Burns, it was the closest that poetry had brought us to such matters. She wore a grey dress and a white apron and a funny white little hat all lost and unbalanced and loveable and comic on the crown of that shining head: her hair was like the links o' gowd, her teeth were like the ivorie, her cheeks like lilies dipped in wine.

—Germany, she said. Switzerland, she said. I couldn't spell Switzerland if you paid me. Germany I can manage.

She did, haltingly, all seven letters, music to mine ears her voice was.

No, she was from Castledawson in County Derry, not too far from where, 33 years later, the meteorite was to splash down, and her family name was Beatty and Trudi came out of a magazine called *Peg's Paper* that her mother read. Her father kept an unlicensed bull that was worth a fortune, he worked so hard, even at half the legal price, but it was cash down for if it wasn't some of them wouldn't pay you at all, you had no legal way of getting at them, and that was about the meanest thing she ever heard of. Cash and carry, her father, who was a joker, said. That was the name of one of those new-fangled supermarkets. On the first morning she told me about Castledawson and Beatty and *Peg's Paper* but it was the third morning, we were rapidly growing closer, before she told me about the unlicensed bull, and laughed like a music box when she told me: You should see him, the solemn face of him.

She was lovelier than the lovely lake in London, lovelier than red sails in the sunset although Fuzzy-Wuzzy would never agree with that and disapproved of Trudi: jealous, I thought at first, but no, I knew after a while that he was just shy of women. It was the red sails in the song that enchanted him, not the loved one that the red sails were to carry home safely to the singer. Bill, a big affable man whose longest speech about anything was a grunt of good-natured assent, was neutral although he did whisper to Fuzzy-Wuzzy to whisper to me that there'd be hell to pay when Busto found out, as find out he sure as hell would, that time was spent helping the lass that made the bed to me that should have been spent in the Presbyterian assembly building in Fisherwick Place outside which, 33 years later, Dr Paisley was picked up for disturbing the peace.

As for Fuzzy-Wuzzy, everywhere he went he must have seen red sails in the sunset. He hummed the tune of it all the time, or something not unlike the tune. He never could make any fist of the words although, God knows, he tried very hard. He was six feet two inches when he was seventeen and he walked on his toes, bouncing a bit, and always leaned forward a little as if he were eager to fly or take off like a rocket for the moon. His real name was Patrick Ignatius O'Kane and his people were far-out relations of my mother, and he wore grey tweed trousers and a serge navy-blue jacket, the jacket always too big for him and the trousers always too small. In the village he came from, we reckoned, there must be a very special tailor, either that or his father had a very large family of boys all older than Fuzzy-Wuzzy. Some in navy-blue serge, others in grey tweed.

Most of our last year at school he spent in Peter Sloper McAleer's bicycle shop trying to learn the words and music of Red Sails in the Sunset. He could, as I've said, make a stab at the music but never, no, no never, he could never get the words right. He cycled into the town to school from his village twelve miles away, so that he had a legitimate reason for being in Peter Sloper's where he parked his bike: and Peter Sloper with his tan shopcoat all marked with streaks of oil, and his small, exactly-oval gold-rimmed spectacles, and his wrinkled monkey-face and his five ribs of grey hair plastered straight across his bald crown, was a man to reckon with. He walked out young nurses from the county hospital until he was the age of 80, nurses, only nurses: the nurses, he used to say with great solemnity, the nurses are the worst, they know it all. My cousin Brigid who was a great deal older than me and who was hospital matron for a time said that it was on the records that Peter Sloper had started walking out nurses when he was eighteen, that was 62 years of young nurses, and never proposed matrimony to one of them which was why he was called Sloper. He was mean, too, or at least tight or careful about money, and never had it been heard of that he bought a drink for anybody except once when a telegram came to him that he had won £50,000 in the Irish Hospitals Sweepstake, and he went crazy and toured the town and bought drinks for one and all and everybody in every pub, to find

out too late that the telegram had come from his best friend, a
greengrocer, who was noted for practical jokes. It was the same
greengrocer who, when Peter Sloper died, suggested that on his
tombstone the words should be cut: The nurses were the worst. But
the parish priest put a stop to that.

Well anyway, there in the middle of a maze and a pop-art swirl
of bicycles was a gramophone with a high green horn playing
music that could be heard two blocks away and Fuzzy-Wuzzy, his
head half up the horn, trying in vain to learn the words of Red Sails
in the Sunset, way out on the sea, oh carry my swift wings straight
home to the shore. Never, oh never could he get the words right:
and he was called Fuzzy-Wuzzy because his hair was black as
coal-tar and bristly and closely clipped.

Bulky affable Bill with a voice like a bugle was such a genius at
Latin composition that his themes or exercises were in constant
demand for what we called cogging and American students rather
grandly called plagiarization. Shakespeare and Eliot plagiarized.
We grimly cogged in the early morning-oh—so that, by popular
request, Bill had to be up early and into the classroom before our
teachers were astir to trouble the air. One morning the demand for
pure Ciceronian Latin was so brisk that a fight began and the
golden book of Bill's themes was torn to shreds. A day of sharp
questioning, discoveries and retribution followed.

—*Festina lente*, Bill said on the third morning in Belfast.

He blushed and looked the other way when he said that. It was
the only attempt he made to reproach me. No, warn me, guide me,
save me, counsel me. He couldn't have reproached anybody: but
dancing with fat waitresses was one thing, dallying in bedrooms
and dereliction of duty that might land the three of us in the
stockade, another. My companions were rattled. Fuzzy-Wuzzy
repeated: *Festina lente*.

But with a sort of shy, awkward half-laugh. And I marvelled
that he was able to get the two words in their right order.

For myself and the blonde belle of Castledawson were into the
straight and ahead of the field, and little was I seeing of the cold,

stone, high-windowed hall where on solemn occasions pious Presbyterians assembled. At one history paper to which I went because
I liked history, and knew how men died and even when, and Trudi
was not that morning available, the man at the next desk to mine
had an epileptic fit and desks and papers and inkwells went flying.
That can't much have affected me: my history marks turned out to
be the best I had when I had any at all.

She taught me to make beds. She taught me to mitre sheets as
neatly as any young nurse ever did in any hospital. She taught me
as the woman lovely in her bones taught the poet: Turn and
Counter-turn and Touch and Stand. The outlaw bull, benevolent,
beneficent in his secret Castledawson meadow, bellowed his blessing: and I taught her a lot about King Charles and Robert Burns.
Not the Charles who lost his head, I assured her, but the Charles
who held on to his head and had all the women he could count.
Like Rudolf Valentino.

—The blackguard.

—Who?

—Both of them. Easy for him and he a king.

—Valentino wasn't a king.

—He was a film-star.

—He died from sleeping with women.

That was a gentlemanly way of putting what we then happily
and enviously believed.

—He should have slept on his own, so.

But it wasn't often that we argued seriously. King Charles on the
run from the Roundheads and the lass, who, according to the
legend and the poem that Robert Burns based on the legend, made
the bed for the fugitive king were better company for us than
Valentino who had it all too easy: I bow'd fu' low unto this maid,
And thank'd her for her courtesie; I bow'd fu' low unto this maid,
And bade her mak a bed to me. . . .

Loftily, and with the style of a man who was a scholar when he
hadn't better things to occupy his mind, I told her: Some people
say that it wasn't about King Charles at all but Robbie Burns
writing about himself and remembering some girl he met in

some inn. He met a lot of girls and wrote a lot of poems about them.

—He was a bit of a playboy, she said. My uncle who's a teacher near Limavady knows a lot about Burns. He was standing in a gateway with a girl, Burns was . . .

She was turning the upper sheet, patting down pillows.

. . . and a wee fellow came by. Eating a bun. And stopped to look. And Robert there and then made a poem: Walk on my son and munch your bun. The works of nature maun be done.

In our places Burns was as much part of the folklore as he was in the land he was born in.

We laughed over the story. We tackled the bed in the next room. Once only had I to run and hide when a stout, supervising, old lady came along. Trudi, while I stood mute in a built-in wardrobe, sang, sweetly and with a Scot's accent as good as real, that her love was like a red red rose. In the darkness I thought: She took her mither's holland sheets, and made them a' in sarks to me. Blythe and merry may she be, the lass that made the bed to me.

Burns and the lass and the king, perhaps, were with us in whatever room we happened to be in. They didn't intrude. They encouraged us in happiness and folly. Long afterwards I read a translation from some Spanish (I think) poet, and knew then what we were up to and, because I couldn't put it better myself, memorised the words: My chosen part to be with a girl and alone with her secret and her gift.

Morning after morning the real true scholars marched off with pen, pencil, ruler, box of mathematical instruments and the accumulated wisdom of the ages to the grim assembly hall. Some of the times I went with them but my heart wasn't in it, my mind wasn't on it. Trudi, whether present or not, was a dream of my early morning and, as I've said, breakfast was perfunctory and the main meal of the day, a very late lunch, was eaten in the Café Continental or the Continental Café when the regulars were fed and back in their shops and offices, and the floor and the air clear for dancing and music. Our examination papers of the day were disposed of by that time and we were free to roam the town, men of the town, and one night even so reckless and led by the great lover who for love had given up learning, as to accost a woman of the town. Not an easy thing to do for the first time, as every gentleman knows. Fuzzy-Wuzzy loitered in the rear, dreaming of red sails, and was useless in the action. Bill, imperturbable, all good nature and prepared to be at least polite, came two paces behind me and I, in the van, pondered on the best, most telling words to begin with. All I could think of was: Miss, could you show us the way to the Great Northern station?

It was past ten o'clock and all the trains long gone.

She didn't even alter her stride. She said: Wee fella, could you show me the way to the Albert Clock.

And walked on. It wasn't a question, or a pretended question. The Albert Clock, high on the most prominent tower in Belfast and beaming like the moon, was 30 yards away from us.

One evening, after music and dancing and bangers and mash, we did the bookstalls and the curio shops in Smithfield market, a Persian bazaar sort of a place, and I bought Johnson's *Lives of the Poets* and Adam Smith's *The Wealth of Nations*. In one of my history text-books I had read that the younger Pitt had read *The Wealth of Nations* and anything the younger Pitt could do I could do better: it was not recorded in the text-book that he had ever tried to accost a girl under the most prominent tower in London, whichever it then was. The Tower, I suppose.

One evening we came out from Eddie Cantor's *Roman Scandals* and saw, in the queue waiting to get in—it was our last day but one in Belfast—Trudi and a young man arm-in-arm and smiling into each other's eyes. They didn't see us. Fuzzy-Wuzzy blushed and said nothing. Oh, carry my loved one home safely to me, we'll marry tomorrow and go sailing no more. Bill said sadly that women were women and it might be that I was her beau only in the early morning. Even for then, beau was a curiously Edwardian word to use. Next morning she told me that it was her cousin from Castledawson and surely to God it was no sin to go to the cinema with her cousin and that, moreover, I'd never asked her out in the evening. Which I had to admit was the bare truth. She had been so much a part of the morning that it had never occurred to me that she might be free in the evening and what, without me, would Bill and Fuzzy-Wuzzy have done, parading the town and lacking their natural leader? We made it up and made the beds and that was the last time but one I saw her.

The starlings may still be there but the old Persian markets are gone, destroyed by bombs. The black news never mentions the starlings.

Lanko was gentle about it when the results came out and Bill and Fuzzy were called and I was not. But he seemed a trifle puzzled, a trifle hurt. There were, after all, three quite inexplicable zeros. Busto huffed and puffed but to my amazement and relief made little comment, and not one place-kick, not one attack on my hair style. But I knew that he knew that something out of the ordinary had happened, that God had saved the king from my services: and he hoped that, for me, something else would turn up.

Those zeros? Well, not quite inexplicable. At least with audacity, *De l'audace, et encore de l'audace, et toujours l'audace*, as the man said who died by the guillotine, with audacity and the aid of friends they could be explained away.

Because three months previously, flogging a mountain stream for trout, in my brother's company and with a triple-hooked bait-tackle that was just about legal, I'd gone in ass first, fished all day in wet clothes and caught one trout, spent three weeks in bed, tossing and turning, my brain tormented, as the brain of man coming out of a bad attack of alcohol might be, by a turning and turning repetition: I would that we were, my beloved, white birds on the foam of the sea.

Over and over and over again. Turning, turning, turning, turning, turning.

Perhaps that had set me in the mood for Trudi, and Bill and Fuzzy-Wuzzy may not have been so far out when they lied like heroes about the flushed and feverish state I'd been in on three Belfast mornings. As heroes I gratefully remember them.

Busto said: Watch it. First in one exam. Twenty-first in the next. Up and down, up and down, watch it, boy.

He may have been a bit of a prophet. For the moment all were happy except my mother who worried about her delicate boy. For a while.

Twice I wrote to Trudi, once to Belfast and once to Castledawson and never had an answer. She couldn't spell Switzerland so that she mightn't have been so good at the writing. Better by far at the making of beds and the mitring of sheets: Her bosom was the drifted snaw, twa drifted heaps sae fair to see; her limbs the polish'd marble stane, the lass that made the bed to me.

And it came to pass that Bill was called to the civil service of the King of England to the city of Carlisle, and then to the army in 1939. After the war (that one) he went into the Palestine police and, after that, to somewhere farther east of Suez and never came home again. Fuzzy-Wuzzy, being called, went to London and its lovely lake and then to the royal navy and, in 1941, sank with a minesweeper in the Channel: oh carry my loved one home safely to me. He never could get the words right.

Flat on my back in a Dublin hospital I heard the news of his death and saw him with his head up the green horn in Peter Sloper's and wondered where I'd be at that moment if Trudi hadn't come between me and the assembly hall: and saw red sails in the sunset and the Rhododendrons round the lovely lake and, through misted eyes, two student nurses mitring my sheet at the corners of my bed: the nurses are the best.

An authority on such things—a man who wrote a book on John McCormack—tells me that the reason why we studied music in bicycle shops was this: the sale of push-bikes in Edwardian times was seasonal, you sold them in the summer. The sale of phonographs and, before them, of the primitive wax cylinders was also seasonal; you sold them in the winter. Bicycle sales, he tells me, thrived during the summer and slumped in winter. Phonographs sold well coming up to Christmas and hardly at all after the festive season. So that, if you were, like Peter Sloper, into both bicycles and phonographs you prospered all the year round and walked the student nurses in your leisure moments.

Where I came from, Edwardian days lasted until 1939.

THERE ARE MEADOWS IN LANARK

The SCHOOLMASTER IN Bomacatall or McKattle's Hut was gloved and masked and at his beehives when his diminutive brother, the schoolmaster from Knockatatawn, came down the dusty road on his high bicycle. It was an Irish-made bicycle. The schoolmaster from Knockatatawn was a patriot. He could have bought the best English-made Raleigh for half the price, but instead he imported this edifice from the Twenty-six into the Six Counties and paid a mountain of duty on it. The bike, and more of its kind, was made in Wexford by a firm that made the sort of mowing-machine that it took two horses to pull. They built the bikes on the same solid principle. Willian Bulfin from the Argentine who long ago wrote a book about rambling in Erin had cycled round the island on one of them and died not long afterwards, almost certainly from over-exertion. There was a great view from the saddle. Hugh, who was the son of the school-master from Bomacatall, once on the quiet borrowed the bike and rode into the side of a motor-car that was coming slowly out of a hedgy hidden boreen. He was tossed sideways into the hedgerow and had a lacework of scratches on his face. The enamel on the car was chipped and the driver's window broken. The bike was unperturbed.

The little man mounted the monster by holding the grips on the handlebars, placing his left foot on the extended spud or hub of the back wheel and then giving an electrified leap. This sunny evening he dismounted by stepping on to the top rail of the garden fence at Bomacatall. He sat there like a gigantic rook, the King Rook that you hear chanting base barreltone in the rookery chorus. He wore a pinstriped dark suit and a black wide-brimmed hat. He paid no attention to the buzzing and swarming of the bees. The herbaceous borders, the diamond-shaped beds at Bomacatall would blind you.

There was a twisting trout stream a field away from the far end of the garden. To his brother who was six feet and more the little man said: I have a scheme in mind.

From behind the mask the big man said: Was there ever a day that God sent that you didn't have a scheme in mind?

—It would benefit the boy Hugh. *Cé an aois é anois?*

That meant: What age is he now?

—Nine, God bless him.

—Time he saw a bit of the world. Bracing breezes, silvery sands, booming breakers, lovely lands: Come to Bundoran.

That was an advertisement in the local newspaper.

—You could sing that if you had a tune to it, said the man behind the mask.

—The holiday would do him good, the King Rook said, and for three weeks there'd be one mouth less to feed.

That was a forceful argument. The master from Knockatatawn, or the Hill of the Conflagrations, was a bachelor. Hugh was midways in a household of seven, not counting the father and mother.

The bees settled. The bee-keeper doffed the mask and wiped the sweat off a broad humorous face. He said: James, like St Paul you're getting on. You want another to guide you and lead you where thou would'st not.

—John, said the man on the fence, in defiance of Shakespeare, I maintain that there are only three stages in a man's life: young, getting-on, and not so bad-considering. I've a sad feeling that I've got to the third.

The nine-year-old, as he told me a long time afterwards, was all for the idea of Bundoran except that, young as he was, he knew there was a hook attached. This was it. At home on the Hill of the Conflagrations there wasn't a soberer man than the wee schoolmaster, none more precise in his way of life and his teaching methods, more just and exact in the administering of punishments or rewards. But Bundoran was for him another world and he, when he was there, was another man. He met a lot of all sorts of people. He talked his head off, behaved as if he had never heard of algebra or a headline copy-book, and drank whisky as if he liked it and as if the world's stock of whisky was going to run dry on the following morning. Yet, always an exact man, he knew that his powers of navigation, when he was in the whisky, were failing, that—as Myles na Gopaleen said about a man coming home from a night at a boat-club dance in Islandbridge—he knew where he was coming from and going to, but he had no control over his lesser movements. He needed a pilot, he needed a tug, or both combined in one: his nephew. There was, also, this to be said for the wee man: he was never irascible or difficult in drink, he went where the pilot guided him and the tug tugged him. He was inclined to sing, but then he was musical and in the school in Knockatatawn he had a choir that was the terror of Féis Doire Cholmcille, the great musical festival held in Derry in memory of St Colmcille. He even won prizes in Derry against the competition of the Derry choirs—and that was a real achievement.

So for one, two, three, four years the nephew-and-uncle navigational co-operation worked well. The nephew had his days on the sand and in the sea. He even faced up to it with the expert swimmers at Roguey Rocks and the Horse Pool. By night while he waited until his uncle was ready to be steered back to the doss he drank gallons of lemonade and the like, and saw a lot of life. With the natural result that by the time the fifth summer came around, that summer when the winds were so contrary and the sea so treacherous that the priest was drowned in the Horse Pool, the nephew was developing new interests: he was looking around for the girls. At any rate, Bundoran or no Bundoran, he was growing up. Now this was a special problem because the schoolmaster from Knockatatawn had little time for girls, for himself or anybody else and, least of all, for his nephew who, in the fifth summer, had just passed thirteen.

One of the wonders of the day on which they helped the schoolmaster from Knockatatawn to the hotel and happed him safely into bed by four o'clock in the afternoon was that Hugh saw a woman, one of the Scotchies, swimming at her ease in the pool where the priest had been drowned. She was a white and crimson tropical fish, more blinding than the handsomest perch in the lake at Corcreevy or the Branchy Wood: white for arms, shoulders, midriff and legs; crimson for cap and scanty costume. Women were not supposed to be in the Horse Pool on any account but so soon after the drowning, the usual people were shunning it, and that woman either didn't know or didn't care. The Scotchies who came to the seaside to Bundoran in the summer had a great name for being wild.

In the hotel bedroom the sun came in as muted slanted shafts through the cane blinds. The shafts were all dancing dust. Carpet-sweepers weren't much in use in that hotel. They helped the wee man out of his grey sober clothes and into a brutal pair of blue-and-white striped pyjamas. He was a fierce hairy wee fellow. Arms long like an ape and a famous fiddler when he was sober. The big purple-faced schoolmaster from Lurganboy said: Begod, you're like a striped earthenware jar of something good.

The little man waved his arms and tried to sing and once slipped off the edge of the bed and sat on the floor and recited word-perfect:

> A Chieftain to the Highlands bound
> Cries: Boatman, do not tarry,
> And I'll give thee a silver crown
> To row me o'er the ferry.

The lot of it, every verse, all about how the waters wild swept o'er his child and how Lord Ullin's daughter and her lover were drowned. The drowning of the priest must have put it into his mind. The purple-faced man from Lurganboy, rocking a little, listened with great gravity, his head to one side, his black bushy eyes glistening, his thick smiling lips bedewed with malt. He said: In the training college he was renowned for his photographic memory. And for the fiddle.

Hugh said nothing. He was sick with delight. His uncle was a blue-and-white earthenware jar of Scotch whisky, as full as it could hold. He always drank Scotch in Bundoran, out of courtesy, he said, to the hundreds of Scotchies who came there every year on their holidays and spent good money in the country. The music of hurdy-gurdies and hobby-horses and the like came drifting to them from the strand, over the houses on the far side of the town's long street. This blessed day the blue-and-white jar could hold no more. He would sleep until tomorrow's dawn and Hugh was a free man, almost fourteen, and the world before him.

—He'll rest now, said the red-faced master from Lurganboy.

They tiptoed out of the room and down the stairs.

—What'll you do now, boy?

—Go for a walk.

—Do that. It's healthy for the young.

He gave Hugh a pound, taken all crumpled out of a trouser pocket. Then nimbly, for such a heavy man, he sidestepped into a raucous bar and the swinging doors, glass, brass and mahogany, closed behind him. It was an abrupt farewell yet Hugh was all for him, and not only because of the crumpled pound, but because in him, man to man and glass for glass, the schoolmaster from the Hill of the Conflagrations had for once taken on more than his match. Several times as they helped the little man towards his bed the unshakeable savant from Lurganboy had said to Hugh: Young man, you are looking at one who in his cups and in his declining years can keep his steps, sir, like a grenadier guard.

He had the map of his day already worked out in his head. The Scotchy girl wouldn't be sitting on the high windowsill until seven o'clock. She was there most evenings about that time. She and God knew how many other Scotchies, male and female, lived in a three-storeyed yellow boarding-house at the east end of the town. There was a garden in front of it, a sloping lawn but no fence or hedge, and the two oval flower-beds were rimmed with great stones, smoothed and shaped by the sea, tossed up on the beach at Tullaghan to the west, gathered and painted and used as ornaments by the local people. This Scotchy girl was one that liked attention. The way she went after it was to clamber out of a bedroom window on the third floor and to sit there for an hour

or more in the evening kicking her heels, singing, laughing, pretending to fall, blowing kisses, and shouting things in unintelligible
Scottish at the people in the street below, throwing or dropping
things, flowers, chocolates, little fluttering handkerchiefs and
once, he had heard, a pair of knickers. He had only seen her once at
those capers when one evening he navigated past, tug before
steamship, with his uncle in tow. But a fella he knew slightly told
him she was to be seen there at that time most evenings. She sure as
God was there to be seen. It wouldn't have been half the fun if she'd
worn a bathing-suit, but a skirt with nothing underneath was
something to tell the fellas about when he got back to Bomacatall.
Not that they'd believe him, but still.

Behind her in the room there must have been 30 girls. They
squealed like a piggery. That was a hell of a house. A randyboo, the
wee master called it. Bomacatall, Knockatatawn and Corcreevy
all combined never heard the equal of the noise that came out of
that house. On the ground floor the piano always going, and a
gramophone often at the same time, and a melodeon and pipes,
and boozy male voices singing Bonny Doon and Bonny Charlie's
noo awa' and Over the sea to Skye and Loch Lomond and The
Blue Bells of Scotland and Bonny Strathyre and Bonny Mary of
Argyle and, all the time and in and out between everything else:

> For I'm no awa tae bide awa,
> For I'm no awa tae leave ye,
> For I'm no awa tae bide awa,
> I'll come back an' see ye.

—They work hard all year, the wee master said. In the big
factories and shipyards of Glasgow. Then they play hard. They're
entitled to it. The Scots are a sensitive generous people and very
musical.

This was the map that was in Hugh's mind when the red- or
purple-faced master from Lurganboy left him outside the swinging
doors of the saloon bar. That Lurganboy man was a wonder to see

at the drink. When he moved, Hugh thought, he should make a
sound like the ocean surf itself with the weight of liquid inside him.
He had also said something remarkable and given Hugh a phrase
to remember. For as they'd steered the Knockatatawn man round
a windy corner from the promenade to the main street, a crowd,
ten or eleven, of Scotchy girls had overtaken them, singing and
shouting, waving towels and skimpy bathing-suits, wearing slacks
and sandals, bright blouses, short skirts, sweaters with sleeves
knotted round their waists and hanging over rumps like britchens
on horses.

—This town, said the master from Lurganboy, is hoaching with
women.

That was the northern word you'd use to describe the way
fingerlings wriggle over and around each other at the shallow
fringes of pools on blinding June days.

—Hoaching. Hoaching with women, Hugh said to himself as he
set out to follow the map he had drawn in his mind that would
bring him back at seven o'clock to the place where the daft girl
kicked her heels and more besides on the windowsill.

From the house of glass to the Nuns' Pool by way of the harbour
where the fishing boats are. It isn't really a house of glass. This
shopkeeper has a fanciful sort of mind and has pebbledashed the
front wall of his place with fragments of broken glass. The shop
faces east, catching the morning sun, the whole wall then lives and
dances like little coloured tropical fish frisking, hoaching, in a giant
aquarium. Hugh can look down on it from his window which is
right on top of the hotel across the street. Some people say the wall
is beautiful. Some people say the man is crazy. The seer from
Knockatatawn says that's the way with people.

Westward the course towards the Nuns' Pool. Passing the place
where the sea crashes right into the side of the street, no houses
here, and only a high strong wall keeps it from splattering the
traffic. Here in the mornings when the tide is ebbed and the water
quiet a daft old lady in a long dress walks out along rocks and sand,
out and out until she's up to her neck in the water, dress and all,

and only her head and wide-brimmed straw hat to be seen. Then she comes calmly out again and walks home dripping. Nobody worries or bothers about her. The bay is her bath tub. She lives here winter and summer.

This day the harbour is empty, a few white sails far out on the bay, pleasure boats. He sits on the tip of the mole for a while and looks down into the deep translucent water. On the gravelly bottom there are a few dead discarded fish, a sodden cardboard box, and fragments of lobster claws turned white. If he could clamber around that sharp rock headland and around two or three more of the same he could peep into the Nuns' Pool and see what they're up to. Do they plunge in, clothes and all, like the mad woman in the morning? It's hard to imagine nuns stripping like the Scotchy in the pool where the priest was drowned. Surely the priests and the nuns should share the one pool and leave Roguey Rocks and the Horse Pool to the men and the wild Scotchies. The strand and the surf are for children and after five summers he knows he's no longer a child.

But he's also alone and he knows it. Tugging and steering his mighty atom of an uncle has taken up all his time and cut him off from his kind. On the clifftop path by the Nuns' Pool there are laughing girls by the dozen, and couples walking, his arm as tightly around her as if she had just fainted and he is holding her up. In corners behind sod fences there are couples asprawl on rugs or on the naked grass, grappled like wrestlers but motionless and in deep silence. Nobody pays the least attention to him. Fair enough, he seems to be the youngest person present. Anyone younger is on the sand or in the surf. Or going for rides on donkeys. He is discovering that, unless you're the tiniest bit kinky, love is not a satisfactory spectator sport.

Steep steps cut in rock go down to the Nuns' Pool. Was it called after one nun or gaggles of nuns, season after season? It must have been one horse. But what was a horse ever doing out there on rocks and seaweed and salt water? He sees as he walks a giant nun, a giant horse. The steep steps turn a corner and vanish behind a wall of rock as big as Ben Bulben mountain. Only God or a man in a helicopter could see what goes on in there. Do they swim in holy silence, praying perhaps, making aspirations to Mary the Star of the Sea? He listens for the sort of shouts and music and screaming laughs that come from the house where the girl sits on the window-sill. He hears nothing but the wash of the sea, the wind in the cliffside grass, the crying of the gulls. What would you expect? It is ten minutes to five o'clock.

He has time to walk on to the place where the Drowes river splits into two and goes to the sea over the ranked, sea-shaped stones of Tullaghan, to walk back to the hotel by the main road, feast on the customary cold ham and tomatoes and tea, bread and butter, wash his hands and face and sleek his hair with Brylcreem and part it up the middle, and still be on good time and in a good place for the seven o'clock show. He does all this. He is flat-footed from walking and a little dispirited. On the stony strand of Tullaghan there isn't even a girl to be seen. If there was he could draw her attention to the wonderful way the sea forms and places the stones, rank on rank, the biggest ones by the water line and matted with seaweed, the smallest and daintiest right up by the sand and the whistling bent-grass. They are variously coloured. The tide has ebbed. Far out the water growls over immovable stones.

He rests for a while by the two bridges over the Drowes river. If there was a girl there he could tell her how the river flows down from Lough Melvin, and how the trout in the lake and the trout in the river have the gizzards of chickens and how, to account for that oddity, there's a miracle story about an ancient Irish saint. There is no girl there. A passing car blinds him with dust. Has the evening become more chilly or is that just the effect of hunger? He accelerates. He knows that while a Scotchy girl might show some interest in stones shaped and coloured into mantelpiece or dressing-room ornaments, she would be unlikely to care much about trout or ancient miracles. In the hotel the master is sound asleep in blue-and-white bars, the bed-clothes on the floor. He doesn't snore. Hugh eats four helpings of ham and tomatoes, two for himself, two for the recumbent fiddler from the Hill of the Conflagrations.

The evening is still ahead of him and the fleshpots delectably steaming. There is no glitter from the house of glass. The hot tea and ham, the thought of the kicking girl on the high windowsill have done him a lot of good. In the evening most of the children will be gone from the strand, the Palais de Danse warming up, the hoaching at its best.

He wasn't the only one watching for the vision to appear, and right in the middle, like a gigantic rugby-football forward holding together a monumental scrum, was the purple-faced man from Lurganboy. The Assyrian, Hugh thought, came down like a wolf on the fold and his cohorts were gleaming in purple and gold. He wasn't his uncle's nephew for nothing, even if he wasn't quite sure what a cohort meant. As he told me long afterwards in the Branchy Wood, or Corcreevy, if his literary education had then advanced as far as *Romeo and Juliet* he would have been able, inevitably, to say: But soft what light through yonder window etc. The man with the face as purple as cohorts saw it differently. To the men that ringed him round he said: Lads, I declare to me Jasus, 'tis like Lourdes or Fatima waiting for the lady to appear. All we lack is hymns and candles.

—We have the hymns, one voice said, she has the candles.

—*Ave ave*, said another voice.

The laughter wasn't all that pleasant to listen to. They were a scruffy enough crowd, Hugh thought, to be in the company of a schoolmaster that had the benefit of education and the best of training; the master from Bomacatall, kind as he was, would have crossed the street if he'd seen them coming. Shiny pointy toes, wide grey flannels, tight jackets, oiled hair; the man from Lurganboy must, at last, like the stag at eve, have drunk his fill or he wouldn't, surely to God, be in the middle of them. Hugh dodged. There was a fine fat flowering bush, white blossoms, bursting with sparrows when the place was quiet, right in the middle of the sloping lawn. He put it between himself and the waiting watching crowd. His back was to the bush. He was very close to the high yellow house. The din was delightful, voices male and female, a gramophone playing a military march, somebody singing that there are meadows in Lanark and mountains in Skye—and he was thinking what a wonderful people the Scots were and what a hell and all of a house that must be to live in, when the high window went up with a bang and there she was, quick as a sparrow on a branch, but brighter, much brighter.

He had heard of a bird of paradise but never had he, nor has he up to the present moment, seen one. But if such a bird exists then its plumage would really have to be something to surpass in splendour what Hugh, in the dying western evening, saw roosting and swinging on the windowsill. Far and beyond Roguey Rocks the sun would be sinking in crimson. The light came over the roofs of the houses across the street, dazzled the windows, set the girl on fire. Long red hair, red dress, pink stockings, red shoes with wooden soles. She was so high up, the angle was so awkward, the late sunlight so dazzling, that he could find out little about her face except that it was laughing. The scrum around the Lurganboy man cheered and whistled. He knew she was laughing, too, because he could hear her. She was shouting down to the Lurganboy contingent, the *caballeros*, but because of the noise from the house and the street he couldn't pick out any words and, anyway, she would be talking Scottish. Nor could he be certain that he had been correctly informed as to what, if anything, she wore underneath the red dress although when he got home to his peers in McKattle's Hut or Bomacatall he sure as God wouldn't spoil a good story by unreasonable doubts.

All told it was an imperfect experience. She twisted and tacked so rapidly, agile as a monkey, that a man could see nothing except crimson. He couldn't even have known that her red shoes had wooden soles if it hadn't been that, with the dink of kicking, one of them came unstuck, and landed as surely as a cricket-ball in his cupped palms where he stood in hiding behind the bush. It was in the pocket of his jacket before he knew what he was doing. Cinderella lost her slipper. He was off through the crowd in a second and nobody but the girl saw him go. The eyes of Lurganboy and his men were on the vision. She screamed high and long. From the far end of the crowd he glanced back and saw her pointing towards him. But nobody bothered to look the way she was pointing. The map of his evening was as clear in his mind as the strand before him, as sure as the shoe in his pocket, and hunt-the-slipper was a game at which anything might happen.

The people in this place have, like the tides, their own peculiar movement. Evening, as he expected, draws most of the children away from the strand to a thousand boarding-house bedrooms. The promise of the moon draws the loving couples, the laughing and shouting groups away from the westward walk by the Nuns' Pool to dry sheltered nooks between strand and dunes, to the hollows in the grassy tops of the high cliffs above Roguey, to the place where later the drums will begin to feel their way in the Palais de Danse. Every night, including Sunday, in the palais there is not only a dance but a few brawls and a talent competition.

No moon yet. No drums yet. The last red rays are drowned in the ocean. The light is grey. The strand is pretty empty and a little chilly, the sea is far out. But as he runs, ankle deep in churned sand, down the slope from the now silent motionless hobby-horses and hurdy-gurdies, he sees a slow, silent procession of people coming towards him around the jagged black corner of Roguey Rocks. The sea washes up almost around their feet. They step cautiously across a shelf of rock, then more rapidly and boldly along the slapping wet sand by the water's edge. Four men in the lead are carrying something. He runs towards them, all girls forgotten. Whatever chance, anyway, he had of meeting a girl during the day he can only have less now in this half-desolate place. The red shoe will be his only souvenir, yet still something to show to the heathens in Bomacatall. Halfways across the strand a distraught woman in shirt and cardigan, hair blowing wild stops him. She says: Wee boy, see if it's a wee boy with fair hair. He's missing for an hour and I'm distracted. Jesus, Mary and Joseph protect him. I'm afraid to look myself.

But it isn't a wee boy with fair hair. It isn't even the crimson-and-white Scotchy girl who had been swimming in the Horse Pool

and whom the sea might have punished for sacrilege, for surely a
dead drowned priest must make some difference to the nature of
the water.

What he sees is nothing that you could exactly put a name to.
The four men carry it on a door taken off its hinges. It's very large
and sodden. There's nothing in particular where the face should
be—except that it's very black. A woman looks at it and gasps.
Somebody says: Cover that up, for God's sake.

A tall red-headed man throws a plastic raincoat over the black
nothing in particular. Hugh walks back to the woman in the skirt
and cardigan. He tells her that it isn't a wee boy with fair hair. She
thanks God.

—It's a big person that must have been a long time in the water.

But she has moved away and isn't listening. He falls in at the tail
of the procession. People leave it and join it, join it and leave it. It's
a class of a funeral. An ambulance comes screaming down the
slope from the long town and parks beside the stabled silent
hobby-horses. Two civic guards come running, a third on a
bicycle. Behind on the strand one single man in a long black coat
walks, fearing no ghosts, towards Roguey Rocks. No couples or
laughing groups are to be seen, even on the grassy clifftops. He
fingers the shoe in his pocket to remind him of girls. A drum
booms, a horn blares from the Palais de Danse which is halfways
up the slope towards the town. He gets in, and for free, simply by
saying that he's singing in Irish in the talent competition.

The hall was already crowded because the evening had turned
chilly and the threat of rain was in the air. He found a seat in a
corner near the ladies where he could watch the procession coming
and going. They came and went in scores and for all the attention
any of them paid to him he might have been invisible. He was
grateful for the anonymity. He was too weary to carry on with the
hopeless chase and that grim vision on the beach had given him
other things to think about. It was still fun to sit and watch the
women, all shapes and sizes and colours, and moods. They went in
demure and came out giggling. That was because most of them, he

had heard, kept noggins of gin and vodka concealed in the cloak-room. It was a great world and all before him. The band was thunderous, the floor more and more crowded until somebody thumped a gong and everybody who could find a chair sat down: girls who couldn't sitting recklessly on the knees of strangers, nobody on his. So he stood up and gave his chair to a girl who didn't even say thanks. The band vanished. A woman sat at the piano, a man with a fiddle and a young fellow with a guitar stood beside her. This was the talent competition.

A grown man long afterwards in the Branchy Wood, or Cor-creevy, he couldn't remember much of it. The time was after eleven, he had been on foot all day, his eyes were closing with sleep. A man with long brown hair and long—the longest—legs and big feet came out, sang in a high nervous tenor about the bard of Armagh, then tripped over the music stand and fell flat on his face. That act was much appreciated. A little girl in a white frock and with spangles or something shining in her hair, tiptoed out, curt-sied, holding the hem of her skirt out wide in her hands, danced a jig to the fiddle, then sang a song in Irish that meant: There are two little yellow goats at me, courage of the milk, courage of the milk. This is the tune that is at the piper, Hielan laddy, Hielan laddy. And more of the same. A fat bald man sang: While I'm jog jog jogging along the highway, a vagabond like me. Then there were tin whistles and concertinas, six sets of Scottish and two of Irish or Uillean pipes, piano accordions, melodeons, combs in tissue paper and clicking spoons, cornet, fiddle, big bass, drum, something, something and euphonium. As the song says.

He lost interest. His insteps ached. He would unnoticed have slipped away only a crowd and girls hoaching was always better than a lonely room. Surveying the crowd from China to Peru he saw in the far corner the man from Lurganboy, like the old priest Peter Gilligan, asleep within a chair, his legs out like logs, hands locked over splendid stomach and watch-chain and velvet waist-coat, chin on chest, black hat at a wild angle but bravely holding on to his head. No angels, as in the case of Peter Gilligan, hovered over him, none that Hugh could see. Five other adults sat in a row beside him, all awake except Lurganboy. Angels that around us hover, guard us till the close of day. Singing that, the Knock-atatawn choir had once won a first prize in Derry city.

As Hugh watched, Lurganboy awoke, pulled in his legs, raised his head, gripped the arms of his chair and hoisted himself to sit erect. The ballroom was silent. Was it the oddness of the silence made the sleeper awake? No, not that, but something, Hugh felt, was going to happen. The drummer was back on the stage. He struck the drum a boom that went round the room, echoing, shivering slowly away. Then the compère said: Ladies and gentlemen.

He said it twice. He held up his right hand. He said again: Ladies and gentlemen, while the judges, including our old, true, tried and stalwart friend from Lurganboy are making up their minds, adding up points, assessing the vast array of talent, not to mention grace and beauty, we will meet again an old friend, a man who needs no introduction, a man who many a time and oft has starred on this stage and who, in days gone by but well remembered has worn more laurels for music than——

The cheers hit the roof, and out on the stage like a released jack-in-the-box stepped the wee master from Knockatatawn, sober as a judge, lively as a cricket, dapper as a prize greyhound, fiddle in one fist, bow in the other. When the cheering stopped he played for fifteen minutes and even the gigglers, resurfacing after gin and vodka, kept a respectful silence. Lord God Almighty, he could play the fiddle.

It could be that the way to get the women is to be a bachelor and play the fiddle, and drink all day and pay no attention to them. For I declare to God, the schoolmaster from Corcreevy said long afterwards, I never saw anything like it before or since, flies round the honeypot, rats round a carcase, never did I see hoaching like that hoaching, and in the middle of it and hopping about on the stage like a wound-up toy, a monkey on a stick, the red Scots girl from the windowsill, and her shoe in my pocket. Radar or something must have told her where it was. She saw me, isolated as I was, standing like a pillar-box in the middle of the floor, for the crowd was on the stage or fighting to get on the stage, and the drum was booming and the compère shouting and nobody listening. She came towards me slowly and I backed away and then ran for the beach, and then stopped. The moon was out between clouds. There was a mizzle of rain.

He stopped running and looked at the moon and the moonlight on the water. This was destiny and he had no real wish to run from it. The moon shines bright, on such a night as this. As he is now, a moonlit beach always reminds him of loneliness, a crowded beach of faceless death. She was a little monkey of a girl and she crouched her shoulders and stooped when she talked. Her red hair was down to her hips. She said: Wee laddie, will ye no gie me backma shoe?

He was learning the language.

—I'm as big as ye are, yersel.

—Will ye no gie me back ma shoe?

She wasn't pleading. She wasn't angry. He knew by her big eyes that it was all fun to her, all part of the holiday. She really wasn't any taller than himself and her foot fitted into his pocket.

—It's no here. It's in ma room.

—You'll bring it tae me.

—For sure. It's no awa tae bide away.

—Guid laddie. Do ye dance?

—Thon's my uncle wi' the fiddle.

—Ye're like him. Ye were quick away wi' ma shoe. I'll no tell him ye're here.

The red shoe was his ticket of admission to the wild happy house. Nothing much, naturally, came of that except a lot of singing and some kisses in the mornings from a sort of elder sister. He learned to talk and understood Scots and to this day, and in his cups, can sing that he's no awa tae bide awa with the best Glaswegian that e'er cam doon frae Gilmour hill. Like his uncle he enjoyed his double life. Not for years, though, not until he had been through college and had his own school, in Corcreevy or the Branchy Wood, did he tell the tale to the old man who by that time was retired and able to drink as he pleased. The old fellow, mellow at the time, laughed immoderately and said: Seemuldoon, I always hold, is a land of milk and honey if you keep your own bees and milk your own cow.

That was a favourite and frequently irrelevant saying of his. Seemuldoon, meaning the dwelling-place of the Muldoons, was, in all truth, the place he came from, and not Knockatatawn. Nor did the man from Lurganboy really come from Lurganboy: I used the name just because I like it, and when people ask me to go to Paris and places like that I say no, I'll go to Lurganboy. Because you don't *go* to Lurganboy, you find yourself there when you lose the road going somewhere else.

BLUEBELL MEADOW

W̲ʜᴇɴ sʜᴇ ᴄᴀᴍᴇ home in the evening from reading in the park
that was a sort of an island the sergeant who had been trounced by
the gipsies was waiting to ask her questions about the bullets. He
had two of them in the cupped palm of his right hand, holding the
hand low down, secretively. His left elbow was on the edge of the
white-scrubbed kitchen table. The golden stripes on his blue-black
sleeve, more black than blue, were as bright as the evening sunshine on the old town outside. He was polite, almost apologetic, at
first. He said: I hate to bother yourself and your aunt and uncle.
But it would be better for everybody's sake if you told me where
you got these things. People aren't supposed to have them. Least of
all girls in a convent school.

There had been six of them. The evening Lofty gave them to her
she had looked at them for a whole hour, sitting at that table,
half-reading a book. Her uncle and aunt were out at the cinema.
She spread the bullets on the table and moved them about, making
designs and shapes and patterns with them, joining them by
imaginary lines, playing with them as if they were draughts or
dominoes or precious stones. It just wasn't possible that such
harmless mute pieces of metal could be used to kill people. Then
she wearied of them, put them away in an old earthenware jug on
the mantelpiece and after a while forgot all about them. They were
the oddest gifts, God knew, for a boy to give to a girl. Not diamonds
again, darling. Say it with bullets.

This is how the park happens to be a sort of an island. The river
comes out of deep water, lined and overhung by tall beeches, and
round a right-angled bend to burst over a waterfall and a salmon
leap. On the right bank and above the fall a sluice-gate regulates
the flow of a millrace. A hundred yards downstream the millrace is

carried by aqueduct over a rough mountain stream or burn coming down to join the river. Between river and race and mountain stream is a triangular park, five or six acres, seats by the watersides, swings for children, her favourite seat under a tall conifer and close to the corner where the mountain stream meets the river. The place is called Bluebell Meadow. The bluebells grow in the woods on the far side of the millrace.

When the river is not in flood a peninsula of gravel and bright sand guides the mountain stream right out into the heart of the current. Children play on the sand, digging holes, building castles, sending flat pebbles skimming and dancing like wagtails upstream over the smooth water. One day Lofty is suddenly among the children just as if he had come out of the river which is exactly what he has done. His long black waders still drip water. The fishing-rod which he holds in his left hand, while he expertly skims pebbles with the right, dips and twiddles above him like an aerial. The canvas bag on his back is sodden and heavy and has grass, to keep the fish fresh, sticking out of the mouth of it. One of the children is doing rifle-drill with the shaft of his net. She has never spoken to him but she knows who he is.

When she tires of reading she can look at the river and dream, going sailing with the water. Or simply close her eyes. Or lean back and look up into the tall conifer, its branches always restless and making sounds, and going away from her like a complicated sort of spiral stairway. She has been told that it is the easiest tree in the world to climb but no tree is all that easy if you're wearing a leg-splint. She is looking up into the tree, and wondering, when Lofty sits beside her. His waders are now dry and rubbery to smell. The rod, the net and the bag are laid on the grass, the heads of two sad trout protruding, still life that was alive this morning. Her uncle who keeps greyhounds argues that fishing is much more cruel than coursing: somewhere in the happy river are trout that were hooked and got away, hooks now festering in their lovely speckled bodies. She thinks a lot about things like that.

Lofty sits for five minutes, almost, before he says: I asked Alec Quigley to tell you I was asking for you.

—He told me.

—What did you say?

—Did he not tell you?

—He said you said nothing but I didn't believe him.

—Why not?

—You had to say something.

—If I said anything Alec Quigley would tell the whole town.

—I daresay he would.

—He's the greatest clatter and clashbag from hell to Omagh.

—I didn't know.

—You could have picked a more discreet ambassador.

The words impress him. He says: It's a big name for Alec Quigley. I never thought of him as an ambassador.

—What then? A go-between? A match-maker? A gooseberry?

They are both laughing. Lofty is a blond tall freckled fellow with a pleasant laugh. He asks her would she like a trout.

—I'd love one. Will we cook it here and now?

—I can roll it in grass for you and get a bit of newspaper in McCaslan's shop up at the waterfall.

—Who will I tell my aunt and uncle gave me the trout?

—Tell them nothing. Tell them you whistled and a trout jumped out at you. Tell them a black man came out of the river and gave you a trout.

He left his bag and rod where they were and walked from the apex of the triangular park to the shop at the angle by the waterfall. He came back with a sheet of black parcelling paper and wrapped up the trout very gently. He had long delicate hands, so freckled that they were almost totally brown. The trout, bloody mouth gaping, looked sadly up at the two of them. Lofty said: I'd like to go out with you.

—I'm often out. Here.

So he laughed and handed her the trout and went on upstream towards the falls, casting from the bank at first, then wading knee-deep across a shallow bar of gravel and walking on across a green hill towards the deeps above the falls. She liked his long stride, and the rod dipping and twiddling above him, and the laden bag—even though she knew it was full of dead gaping trout. She knew he was a popular fellow in the town. Yet she didn't tell her aunt and uncle who exactly it was had made her a gift of the trout. She said it was an elderly man and she wasn't quite sure of his name, but she described him so that they'd guess he was a well-known fisherman, a jeweller by trade and highly respected in the town. Not that Lofty and his people were disrespectable.

The gipsies who trounced the sergeant hadn't been real romany gipsies but tinkers or travelling people from the west of Ireland, descendants, the theory was, of broken people who went on the roads during the hungry years of the 1840s and hadn't settled down since. Five of them, wild, ragged, rough-headed fellows came roaring drunk out of a pub in Bridge Lane. The pub was owned by a man called Yarrow and the joke among those literate enough to appreciate it was about Yarrow Visited and Yarrow Revisited. There was also an old English pishroge about girls putting Yarrow, the plant, between two plates and wishing on it and saying: Good morrow, good morrow, good yarrow, thrice good morrow to thee! I hope before this time tomorrow thou wilt show my true love to me.

One of the five fell with a clatter down the three steps from the door of the pub. In their tottering efforts to pick him up two of the others struck their heads together and began to fight. The remaining two joined in and so, when he was able to stand up, did the fellow who had fallen down the steps. The sergeant was walking past and was fool enough to try to stop them. In the west of Ireland the civic guards had more sense and stood as silent spectators until the tinkers had hammered the fight out of each other.

The five of them, united by foreign invasion, gave the sergeant an unmerciful pounding. He had just enough breath left to blow his whistle. More police came running. More tinkers came shouting, men, women and children, out of the pub, out of dark tunnels of entryways between houses, out of holes in the walls. The battle escalated. More police came. The tinkers made off on two flat carts. One old man was so drunk he fell helpless off a cart and was arrested. The police followed in a tender.

At their encampment of caravans a mile outside the town the tinkers abandoned the carts and took in the darkness to the fields and the hedgerows and even, it was said, to the tops of the trees. The police wisely did not follow, but set a heavy guard on the camp, caravans, carts, horses, scrap metal and everything the tinkers owned. Sober and sheepishly apologetic they reappeared in the morning and gave themselves up and half a dozen of them went to jail. But for a long time afterwards when the sergeant walked the town the wits at the street-corner would whistle: Oh, play to me gipsy, the moon's high above.

Thanks to Arthur Tracy, known as the Street Singer, it was a popular song at the time.

In spite of all that, the sergeant remained an amiable sort of man, stout, slow-moving, with a large brown moustache and a son who was a distinguished footballer.

Yarrow is a strong-scented herb related to the daisies. It has white or pink flowers in flat clusters.

One Sunday in the previous June in an excursion train to Bundoran by the western sea she had overheard Lofty's mother telling funny stories. As a rule Protestants didn't go west to Bundoran but north to Portrush. The sea was sectarian. What were the wild waves saying: At Portrush: Slewter, slaughter, holy water, harry the papishes every one, drive them under and bate them asunder, the Protestant boys will carry the drum. Or at Bundoran: On St Patrick's day, jolly and gay, we'll kick all the Protestants out of the way, and if that won't do we'll cut them in two and send them to hell with their red, white and blue.

Nursery rhymes.

She sat facing her aunt in the train and her uncle sat beside her. They were quiet, looking at all the long beauty of Lough Erne which has an island, wooded or pastoral, for every day in the year. Her aunt, a timid little woman, said now and again: Glory be to God for all his goodness.

Her uncle said just once: You should see Lake Superior. No end to it. As far as the human eye can see.

Then they were all quiet, overhearing Lofty's mother who had no prejudices about the religion of the ocean and who, with three other people, sat across the corridor from them, and who had a good-natured carrying voice and really was fun to listen to. She was saying: I'm a Protestant myself, missus dear, and I mean no disrespect to confession but you must have heard about the young fellow who went to the priest to tell him his sins and told him a story that had more women in it than King Solomon had in the Bible and the goings-on were terrible, and the priest says to him, Young man are you married?, and the young fellow says back to him, dead serious and all, Naw father but I was twice in Fintona.

The train dived through a tunnel of tall trees. The lake vanished. Sunlight flashing and flickering through leaves made her close her eyes. Everybody on the train, even her aunt, seemed to be laughing. A man was saying: Fintona always had a bit of a name. For wild women.

Lofty's mother said, I was born there myself but I never noticed that it was all that good, nobody ever told me.

She opens her eyes and the sunlight flickers down on her through the spiralling branches of the great conifer. There's a book in the public library that has everything, including pictures, about all the trees of Great Britain and Ireland. Lofty is on the very tip of the peninsula of sand and gravel, demonstrating fly-casting to half a dozen children who are tailor-squatting around his feet. She is aware that he's showing off to impress her and the thought makes her warm and pleased, ready to laugh at anything. But to pretend that she's unimpressed she leans back and looks up into the tree in which the sunlight is really alive, creeping round the great bole, spots of light leaping like birds from one branch to another. She thinks of the omú tree which grows on the pampas of South America. Its trunk can be anything up to 40 or 50 feet thick. The wood is so soft that when cut it rots like an over-ripe melon and is useless as firewood. The leaves are large, glossy and deep green like laurel leaves—and also poisonous. But they give shade from the bare sun to man and beast, and men mark their way on the endless plains by remembering this or that omú tree. She has read about omú trees. Her own tree is for sure not one of them. She sits up straight when her book is lifted from her lap. Lofty is sitting by her side. The children are pointing and laughing. He must have crept up on hands and knees pretending to be a wild animal, a wolf, a prowling tiger. He's very good at capers of that sort. His rod and net lie by the side of the burn.

It was April when he first sat beside her. It is now mid-June. Her school will close soon for the holidays and she will no longer be compelled to wear the uniform: black stockings, pleated skirt of navy-blue serge, blue gansey, blue necktie with saffron stripes, blue blazer with school crest in saffron on breast-pocket, blue beret, black flat-heeled shoes. Even Juliet, and she was very young, didn't have to wear a school uniform. If she had had Romeo wouldn't have looked at her.

Not that they are star-crossed lovers or Lofty any Romeo. They haven't even crossed the millrace to walk in the bluebell woods as couples of all ages customarily do. She isn't shy of walking slowly because of the leg-splint but she knows that Lofty hasn't asked her because he thinks she might be: that makes her feel for him as she might feel, if she had one, for a witless younger brother who's awkward. And a bit wild: for a lot of Lofty's talk doesn't go with the world of school uniforms mostly blue for the mother of God. What the saffron is for, except variety of a sort, she can't guess. Lofty's rattling restless talk would lift Mother Teresa out of her frozen black rigidity.

Lofty with great good humour fingers the saffron stripes and says that, in spite of everything, she's a wee bit of an Orange-woman. They hold hands regularly. Lofty can read palms, a variant reading every time. They have kissed occasionally, when the children who are always there have been distracted by a water-hen or rat or leaping fish or a broken branch or an iceberg of froth from the falls.

—Don't look now, he says one day, but if you swivel round slowly you'll see my three sisters in action.

Beyond the millrace and against the fresh green of woods she can see the flash of coloured frocks, the glint of brass buttons and pipe-clayed belts. In those days it was only the wild ones who went with the soldiers: it wasn't money and security they were after.

—They're hell for soldiers, he says, between the three of them they'd take on the Germans.

Lofty himself reads a lot of military books, campaigns and generals, Napoleon and Ludendorf, all the way from Blenheim to the Dardanelles. When he doodles as he often does on the writing-pad she always carries with her—to make notes on her reading, to transcribe favourite poems—he doodles uniforms, every detail exact. Yet he listens to her when she reads poetry or the splendid prose of a volume of selected English essays, Caxton to Belloc.

—They're advancing on us, he says. They have us surrounded, enfiladed, debouched and circumnavigated.

—We'll tell Maryanne, the three sisters say, that you're with another.

Two of them, Mildred and Rosemary, are plump, laughing, blonde girls, and Mildred who is the youngest is as freckled as her brother. Gertie, the eldest, is olive-faced, with jet-black hair, wrinkles on the forehead and around the eyes like her mother. She is never to see the father of the family but the gossip of the town is to tell her that he's away a lot in Aldershot and India and that Lofty's mother, that merry woman, is friendly with more soldiers than the one she's married to.

The three British soldiers who are with the sisters are, one of them from Sligo, one from Wexford and one actually from Lanca-shire, England. They all talk and laugh a lot and she likes them. The Lancashire lad climbs right up to the top of the tree and pretends to see everything that's going on in the town and tells them about it: he has a lurid imagination. Then they go away towards the waterfall, still laughing, calling back about telling Maryanne. She asks him who Maryanne is. Lofty who clearly likes his sisters is not in the least embarrassed by the suggestion that he has another woman.

—Oh Maryanne's nobody or nobody much.

—She has a name. She must be somebody.

She's not really jealous, just curious.

—Maryanne's a girl I met one day on the road beyond McCaslan's shop.

—You met nobody on the road?

—She was wheeling a pram.

—She's married to Mr Nobody?

—It wasn't her pram. She's the nursemaid in Mooney's, the fancy-bread bakery. There was a lovely smell of fresh bread.

—Had you a good appetite, apple-jelly, jam-tart?

But since the rest of that rhyme to which children, Protestant and Catholic, rope-skip on the streets, is tell me the name of your sweetheart, she doesn't finish it and finds herself, to her annoyance, blushing. Lofty doesn't seem to notice.

—There were twins in the pram. I pushed it for her up the hill to the main road. Then she said I bet you wouldn't do that for me if it was in the town on the court-house hill where everybody could see you. I said why not and she said Christian Brothers' boys are very stuck-up, I've met some that would do anything they could or you'd let them if they had a girl in the woods or in the dark, but that wouldn't be seen talking to her on the street, maids aren't good enough for them. I didn't tell her I was a Presbyterian and went to the academy.

—Why not?

—She mightn't like a Presbyterian pushing her pram.

They laugh at that until the playing children turn and look and laugh with them. Cheerful voices call from beyond the millrace where soldiers and sisters are withdrawing to the woods.

—We have girls at the academy, on the house, what Harry Cassidy and Jerry Hurst and the boys don't have at the Brothers. Harry and the boys are mad envious when we tell them about the fun we have feeling Daisy Allen under the desk at school. All lies of course.

—I hope Daisy Allen doesn't hear that.

—Och Daisy, she's well handled anyway, she's going about with a bus-driver and he's a married man as well, he ruined a doctor's daughter in Dungannon. Harry and the Catholic boys think the Protestant girls are wilder because they don't have to tell it all in confession. That isn't true either.

One other funny story she had heard Lofty's mother telling that day as the train in the evening left Bundoran station and the great romantic flat-topped mountains diminished into the distance. This time the story-teller faced her aunt and sat beside her uncle who had been talking about jerry-building in a new housing estate. Lofty's mother agreed with him. She had a shopping-bag of sugar to smuggle back into the Six Counties where it cost more. The sugar was tastefully disguised under a top-dressing of dulse. With content and triumph Lofty's mother sang a parody popular at the time: South of the border down Bundoran way, that's where we get the Free State sugar to sweeten our tay.

She was great fun. She had bright blue eyes and a brown hat with a flaring feather, and a brown crinkly face. She said: Those houses are everything you say and worse. Fancy fronts and ready to fall. When you flush the lavatory in them the noise is heard all over the town. Only the other day the lady who lives in number three sent down to River Row for old Mr Hill, the chimney-sweep, and up he came and put the brush up the chimney and then went out, the way sweeps do, to see if the brush was showing out of the top of the chimney. No brush. In he went and screws on another length of handle on the brush and pushes for dear life, and out again to look, but no brush. In again and screws on the last bit of handle he has, and he's pushing away when the lady from number eleven knocks on the door. Have you the sweep in, missus dear, she says. I have, missus dear, says the lady from number three. Then please ask him to be careful, missus dear, she says, that's twice now he's upset our wee Rosy from the lavatory seat.

Because of her happy carrying voice passers-by in the corridor stop to join the fun. The smuggled sugar is safely across the border.

Remembering Lofty's laughing mother makes it easier still to like Lofty. The three sisters also look as if they'd be good for a lot of laughs.

Her uncle is a tall broad-shouldered man with a good grey suit, a wide-brimmed hat, two gold teeth and a drawl. Years ago he was in the building trade in the United States and knows a lot about jerry-building. He gets on very well with Lofty's mother.

It was well on towards the end of August when the black man sat on the bench beside her. She was looking sideways towards the bridge over the millrace, and laughing: because two big rough young fellows were running like hares before Mr McCaslan's boxer dog. Mr McCaslan who owned the shop was also water-bailiff and park-keeper. The rough fellows had been using, brutally, one of the swings meant for small children, so brutally that the iron stays that supported it were rising out of the ground. Mr McCaslan had mentioned the matter to them. They had been offensive, even threatening, to the old rheumatic man so he hobbled back to his shop and sent the boxer dog down as his deputy. The pair took off as if all hell were behind them. It was funny because the dog didn't bark or growl or show hostility, didn't even run fast, just loped along with a certain air of quiet determination and wouldn't (as far as she knew) savage anybody. But he was a big dog even for a boxer and the retreat of the miscreants was faster than the Keystone Cops. She laughed so much that the book fell on the grass. The black man picked it up and sat down beside her.

She thought of him as a black man not because he was a Negro but because her uncle had told her that he was a member of the black preceptory which was a special branch of the Orange Order. She had seen him walking last twelfth of July in the big parade in memory of the battle of the Boyne, which happened a long time ago, and in honour of King William of Orange who was a long time dead and had never been in this town. He had worn the black sash, with shining metallic esoteric insignia attached, as had the other men who marched beside him. The contingent that followed wore blue sashes and were supposed to be teetotallers but her uncle said

that that was not always so. One of the blue men, a red-faced
red-headed fellow was teetering and might have fallen if he hadn't
been holding on to one of the poles that supported a banner.

The drums drummed, the banners bellied in the breeze, the
pipes and fifes and brass and accordions played:

> It is old but it is beautiful
> And its colours they are fine,
> It was worn at Derry, Aughrim,
> Enniskillen and the Boyne.
> My father wore it in his youth,
> In bygone days of yore,
> And· on the Twelfth I'll always wear
> The sash my father wore.

The name of the black man who sat beside her was Samuel
McClintock and he was a butcher. It was said about him for laughs
that if the market ran out of meat the town could live for a week on
McClintock's apron: blue, with white stripes. That August day
and in the public park he naturally wasn't wearing the apron. He
had a black moustache, a heavy blue chin, a check cloth-cap,
thick-soled boots, thick woollen stockings and whipcord knee-
breeches. The Fomorians, the monsters from stormy seas had,
each of them, one arm, one leg and three rows of teeth. He said:
The dog gave those ruffians the run.

The way he said it took the fun out of it. She said: Yes, Mr
McClintock.

She wished him elsewhere. She half-looked at her book. She was
too well-reared to pick it up from her lap and ostentatiously go on
reading. The river was in a brown fresh that day, the peninsula of
sand and gravel not to be seen, nor Lofty, nor the children. The
black man said: Plenty water in the river today.

She agreed with him. It was also a public park in a free-and-
easy town and everyone had a right to sit where he pleased. Yet
this was her own seat under the tall tree, almost exclusively
hers, except when Lofty was there. The black man said: The

Scotchies have a saying that the salmon's her ain when there's water but she's oors when it's oot.

He explained: That means that often they're easier to catch when the water's low.

He filled his pipe and lighted it. The smell of tobacco was welcome. It might have been her imagination but until he pulled and puffed and sent the tobacco smell out around them she had thought that the resinous air under the tree was polluted by the odours of the butcher's shop and apron. He said that the salmon were a sight to see leaping the falls when they went running upstream. She said that she had often watched them.

—I'm told you're very friendly with a well-known young fisherman of my persuasion.

—Who, for instance?

—You know well. That's what I want to talk to you about. It's a serious matter.

—Being friendly with a fisherman?

—Don't play the smarty with me, young lassie. Even if you do go to the convent secondary school. Young people now get more education than's good for them. Lofty at the academy and you at the convent have no call to be chumming it up before the whole town.

—Why not?

But it occurred to her that they hadn't been chumming-up or anything else before the whole town. What eyes could have spied on them in this enchanted island?

—His uncle's a tyler, that's why.

—I never knew he had an uncle.

—His mother's brother is a tyler and very strict.

—What's a tyler?

—I shouldn't repeat it, lassie. But I will, to impress on you how serious it is. A tyler he is and a strict one. Wasn't it him spoke up to have Lofty let into the B Specials?

—Don't ask me. I never knew he was a B Special.

But one day for a joke, she remembered, he had given her a handful of bullets.

—The nuns wouldn't tell you this at school but the B Specials were set up by Sir Basil Brooke to hold Ulster against the Pope and the Republic of Ireland.

The nuns, for sure, hadn't told her anything of the sort: Mother Teresa who was very strong on purity and being a lady and not sitting like a man with your legs crossed had never once mentioned the defensive heroisms of the B Specials who, out in country places, went about at night with guns and in black uniforms, holding up Catholic neighbours and asking them their names and addresses—which they knew very well to begin with. The Lofty she knew in daylight by this laughing river didn't seem to be cut out for such nocturnal capers.

—If his uncle knew that the two of you and you a Catholic girl were carrying-on there'd be hell upon earth.

—But we're not carrying-on.

—You were seen kissing here on this bench. What's that but carrying-on?

—What does he level?

—What does who level?

—The uncle who's a leveller or whatever you called him.

—Speak with respect, young lassie. A tyler, although I shouldn't tell you the secret, is a big man in the Order at detecting intruders. His obligation is this: I do solemnly declare that I will be faithful to the duties of my office and I will not admit any person into the lodge without having first found him to be in possession of the financial password or without the sanction of the Worshipful Master of the Lodge.

Then after a pause he said with gravity: And I'm the worshipful master.

He was the only one of the kind she had ever met or ever was to meet and she did her best, although it was all very strange there by the river and the rough stream and under the big tree, to appear impressed, yet all she could think of saying was: But I'm not interfering with his tyling.

Then she was angry and close to tears, although it was also funny: For all I care he can tile the roofs and floors and walls of every house in this town.

The big man hadn't moved much since he sat down, never raised his voice, but now he shouted; Lassie, I'll make you care. The B Specials are sworn to uphold Protestant liberty and beat down the Fenians and the IRA.

—I'm not a Fenian nor an IRA.

—You're a Roman Catholic, aren't you? And there isn't any other sort. Sir Basil Brooke says that Roman Catholics are 100 per cent disloyal and that he wouldn't have one of them about the house.

—Sir Who's It?

—No cheek, lassie. Didn't he sit up a tree at Colebrook all night long with a gun waiting for the IRA to attack his house? Didn't he found the B Specials to help the police to defend the throne and the Protestant religion?

What was it to her if Sir Somebody or Other spent all his life up a tree at Colebrook or anywhere else? The Lancashire soldier had climbed her tree and been as comic as a monkey up a stick. The black man calmed himself: Your own clergy are dead set against mixed marriages.

—We weren't thinking of marriage.

—What of then? Silliness and nonsense. The young have no wit. What would Mother Teresa say if she heard you were keeping company with a Protestant?

—Who would tell her?

—I might. For your own good and for Lofty.

He knocked the ash out of his pipe and put it away. The pleasant tobacco smell faded. She smelled blood and dirt and heard screams and knew, with a comical feeling of kindness, that she had been wrongly blaming him for bringing with him the stench of the shambles. There was a piggery at the far end of the field beyond the river and the wind was blowing from that direction.

—That's the piggery, she said. It's a disgrace.

—Time and again I've said that on the town council. You must have read what I said in the papers. It's a sin, shame and scandal to have a piggery beside a beauty spot. Not that I've anything against pigs, in my business, in their own place.

He stood up and patted her on the shoulder. He was really just a big rough friendly man: You don't want him put out of the Specials or the Lodge itself.

—Why should he be?

—These are deep matters. But they tell me you read a lot. You've the name for being one of the cleverest students in this town, Protestant or Catholic. So I'll talk to you, all for the best, as if you were a grown-up and one of my own. It is possible but very difficult for a convert to be accepted as a member of the Orange Order.

He was as good as standing to attention. He was looking over her head towards the waterfall.

—A convert would have to be of several years standing and his background would have to be carefully screened. His admission would have to be authorized by the Grand Lodge. They'd have to go that high, like Rome for the Catholics. No convert can get into the Black Preceptory if either of his parents is still living, in case the Roman Catholic Church might exert pressure on a parent.

He was reciting. Like the sing-song way in which in school the children learned the Catechism.

Q: What are the seven deadly sins?
A: Pride, covetousness, lust, gluttony, envy, anger and sloth.
Q: What are the four sins that cry to heaven for vengeance?
A: Wilful murder, sodomy, oppression of the poor and defrauding the labourer of his wages.

Dear Sacred Heart it was a cheery world.

—A convert who was even a Protestant clergyman was blacked-out because one of his parents was still living, and there is automatic expulsion for dishonouring the Institution by marrying a Roman Catholic.

The great tree creaked its branches above them. The brown water tumbled on towards the town.

—You see what I mean, lassie.

She supposed she saw. In a way she was grateful. He was trying to help. He shook her hand as if they were friends forever. He went off towards the waterfall so that, without turning around, she could not see him walking away and he could not, thank God, see her face laughing, laughing. For, sweet heart of Jesus fount of love and mercy to thee we come thy blessings to implore, but it was comic to think of him marching up the convent grounds (he should wear his black sash and have a fife and drum before him) holy white statues to left and right and a Lourdes grotto as high as Mount Errigal, to relate all about the love-life of Lofty and herself to Mother Teresa who had a mouth like a rat-trap—and a mind. A worshipful master and a most worshipful reverend mother and never, or seldom, the twain shall meet. She was an odd sort of a girl. She sat around a lot and had read too many books. It was funny, also, to think of his daughter, Gladys, a fine good-natured brunette with a swinging stride, a bosom like a Viking prow, and a dozen boy friends of all creeds and classes. Nothing sectarian about Gladys who was one of his own kind and the daughter of a worshipful master. Somebody should tell the tyler to keep an eye on her. But she was too clever to be caught, too fast on her feet, too fast on her feet.

Walking slowly past the Orange hall on the way home she thought that the next time she met him she would have a lot to tell to lazy, freckled, lovable Lofty. The Orange hall was a two-storeyed brownstone building at a crossroads on the edge of the town. High on its wall a medallion image of William of Orange on an impossibly white horse rode forever across the Boyne. The two old cannon-guns on the green outside had been captured from the Germans in the Kaiser war. In there, Lofty's lodge met and it was a popular joke that no man could become a member until he rode a buck goat backwards up the stairs. Sometimes in the evenings bands of music played thunderously in there, practising for the day in July when they marched out, banners flying. It was crazy to think that a man on a white horse, riding across a river 200 years ago could now ride between herself and Lofty. Or for that mat-ter—although Mother Teresa would have a fit if she thought that a pupil of hers could think of such things—another man on a chair or something being carried shoulder-high in the city of Rome.

All this she meant to mention to Lofty the next time he came to the seat under the tree. But all she could get around to saying was: Lofty, what's a tyler?

He had no rod and net and was dressed, not for fishing, in a new navy-blue suit. The children called to him from the gravel but he paid no attention to them. At first he didn't pretend to hear her, so she asked him again. He said that a tyler was a man who laid tiles. That was the end of that. Then it was winter. One whole week the park was flooded. She couldn't exactly remember when it was that Lofty had given her the bullets.

It was also crazy to think that Lofty's laughing mother could have a brother who went about spying on people and nosing them out. What eyes had spied on Lofty and herself on the enchanted island? What nosy neighbour had told somebody who told somebody who told the sergeant that she had bullets in the earthenware jug?

—If you don't tell me, the sergeant says, it will be awkward for all concerned. What would Mother Teresa think if she thought you had live bullets in an earthenware jug?

It wasn't possible to control the giggles. What, in the holy name of God, would Mother Teresa think, if the sergeant and the worshipful master descended on her simultaneously, what would she say, how would she look? Keeping live bullets in a jug must be one of the few things that she had not warned her girls against.

—You'll have to come down to the barracks with me. I'll walk ahead and you follow just in case the people are passing remarks. They might think I'm arresting you.

—What are you doing?

—Och, I'd just like you to make a statement. It's not a crime to have bullets. Not for a young lady like you who wouldn't be likely to be using them. But we have a duty to find out where they came from. My son Reggie speaks highly of you, Reggie the footballer you know.

She knew. It was a town joke that the sergeant couldn't speak to anybody for ten minutes without mentioning Reggie who parted his hair up the middle, wore loud scarves and played football very well: it was clear that the sergeant thought that to be thought well of by Reggie was a special distinction.

Old low white houses line the hill that goes up from the brook and the co-operative creamery to the centre of the town. The sergeant plods on, twenty yards ahead of her. The town is very quiet. His black leather belt creaks and strains to hold him together. The butt of his pistol, his black baton case shine. She has never noticed before that Lofty has a stutter. Another sergeant sits behind a desk in the dayroom and makes notes. Two young constables are laughing in the background. The black man comes in and says: I warned the two of them.

Her own sergeant says: There wasn't much harm in it.

—Not for the girl, says the man behind the desk. But for him a breach of discipline.

Lofty has surely never stuttered when he talked to her by the meeting of the waters.

—Did you tell them I gave you the bullets?

—Dear God, it wasn't a crime to give me bullets.

—Did you tell them?

—I did not.

—They said you did.

—So.

Her own sergeant looks ashamed and rubs his moustache. The other sergeant says: Case closed.

Then her uncle walks in, and so hopping mad that he seems to have a mouthful of gold teeth. He talks for a long time and they listen respectfully because he's a famous man for keeping running dogs which he feeds on brandy and beef. He says over and over again: You make a helluva fuss about a few bullets.

—A breach of discipline, says the man behind the desk.

—My ass and yours, says her uncle. A helluva fuss.

And repeats it many times as they walk home together.

—But all the same they'll put him out of the Specials, he says.

And I dare say he shouldn't have been assing around giving away government issue.

Over the supper table he remembers the time he had been a policeman in Detroit: Some Negro trouble then and this rookie policeman from Oklahoma was on patrol with a trained man. The rookie has no gun. So they're rushed by twenty black men and the first rock thrown clobbers the trained man unconscious. But the Oklahoma guy he stoops down, takes the pistol out of the other man's holster and shoots six times and kills six black men, one, two, three, four, five, six. He didn't waste a bullet.

—Sacred Heart have mercy, says her aunt.

—What did the other black men do, uncle?

—They took off for home and small blame to them. He was a cool one, that rookie, and a damned good shot. Here in this place they make a helluva fuss over a few bullets. I told them so.

Lofty came never again to the tall tree. They met a few times on the street and spoke a few words. She left the town after a while and went to work in London. Once, home on holidays, she met Lofty and he asked her to go to the pictures, and she meant to but never did. The Hitler war came on. She married an American and went to live in, of all places, Detroit. Her uncle and aunt and the sergeant and the worshipful master and the tyler and, I suppose, Lofty's mother and old McCaslan and his dog died.

Remembering her, I walked, the last time I was in the town to revisit Bluebell Meadow. The bridge over the millrace was broken down to one plank. Rank grass grew a foot high over most of the island. The rest of it was a wide track of sand and gravel where the river in fierce flood had taken everything before it. The children's swings and all the seats were gone, smashed some time before by reluctant young soldiers from the North English cities doing their national service. Repair work had been planned but then the bombings and murders began.

No laughing Lancashire boy in British uniform will ever again climb the tall tree. For one thing the tree is gone. For another the soldiers go about in bands, guns at the ready, in trucks and armoured cars. There are burned-out buildings in the main streets—although the great barracks is unscathed—and barricades and checkpoints at the ends of the town. As a woman said to me: Nowadays we have gates to the town. Still, other towns are worse. Strabane which was on the border and easy to bomb is a burned-out wreck. And Newry, where the people badly needed shops and factories, and not ruins. And Derry is like Dresden on the day after.

When I wrote to her about this she said, among other things, that she had never found out the name of that tall conifer.

A COW IN THE HOUSE

THERE WAS SOMETHING different and a little disconcerting
about Harry the Barber, possibly because he drank and had a red
face and his hand shook and he kept a cow in the house. The only
other man I had ever heard of who kept animals in his dwelling-
place was a one-eyed, story-book giant who lived in a cave and
came to a bad end. So I went cold all over the Friday morning my
mother told me to trot down the town to Harry's and take fourpence with me and ask him to trim my hair. Up to that fatal
moment, when manhood opened before me like an abyss, my
mother herself had done what barbering I needed: combing, snip-
ping and trimming while I, my eyes tightly closed against
detached, descending hairs, and robed, like a pantomime Bedouin,
in a bath towel, stood on a kitchen chair.

I pleaded: Couldn't you trim my hair yourself? You did it last
Saturday.

—You're big enough now to need a real barber. You're like a
rabbit hiding under a bush.

The giant had roared loudly enough to shatter the roof when the
burning stake plunged into his only eye.

I said: Harry the Barber keeps a cow in the house.

—Isn't he the lucky man to have a cow?

—Wouldn't you like to go with your father, she said, and see the
capital city and visit Sister Barbara in the Nazareth Home?

My mother was all flour. That's how I knew so well it was Friday
morning for Friday morning was three things: our big weekly
baking, particularly of treacle scones which my father loved; the
busiest milk delivery day at the co-operative creamery up the road
past our house; the day they shod cartwheels across the road and
below our terrace on the space of waste ground before Hamilton's
smithy. My mother, white as a snowman, stood baking at a table

where she could look out of a kitchen window and see the farmers' carts, laden with jingling silvery cans, passing up and down the road; and see the smoke and steam rising as the red-hot metal hoops were fitted on to the wooden wheels and then cooled and contracted with cold water.

The three Hamiltons were giants of men: the white-headed father, the tall dark-visaged sons with deep creases in their faces to catch and hold the smoke and soot of the forge. They swung and stooped over the ancient process, setting alight the circle of peat around the iron hoop, blowing the flames with hand-bellows, dragging out with a huge tongs the sparking crimson circle, fitting it to the wood and skilfully applying the rhythmical hammers. But they had six kind eyes between them and they didn't keep cows in the smithy. They had a horse but they kept him decently, housed, bedded and cleaned out, in a stable in Tansey the carter's yard at the end of the town.

My mother laid the foundations for yet another scone. The carts shone and jingled up and down the road. Smoke of singed wood, and steam from the cooled iron arose like a mushroom.

So, for all those reasons, it was Friday morning, but for me the light had gone out of the sunshine. Inching towards the door I said: I'll go look at the Hamiltons.

—You'll go off to Harry the Barber's for a new hair-style. Don't you want to see the capital city of Ireland? Your father says it's time you saw a bit of the world.

—I saw it all in school. It's a shiny round ball. It spins when you touch it.

—You're too clever for your years.

But, in spite of the flour, I could see she was proud of my wit; and I was wise enough to know that going to the capital meant a long glorious journey by train and something to boast about for life. No boy in Primer, which was my grade at school, had ever been further in a train than the mere 40 miles to the sea at Bundoran. Between me and the delights of the long journey to Dublin stood the monster I must pass; the shaking red-faced barber and the cow that would startlingly step out of the hall-door. There was nothing for it but to close my eyes and fare forward. By ill-luck I didn't wear my cap.

A cow's floppy cloven hooves were never made for a hard pavement. Slithering clumsily, the red creature emerged and crossed the footwalk to the street. The shop-door closed behind her and the bell fixed at the top of it jangled. To my alarm she swung her head sideways and looked at me out of enormous eyes. She had a crumpled horn, like the cow that was milked by the maiden all forlorn, and wisps of hay which she was champing at, meditatively, stuck out of the corners of her mouth and wiggled like cats' whiskers. No maiden, forlorn or otherwise, drove the beast from the byre in the barber's backyard to the pasture at the edge of the town. But behind her walked one of the barber's children: a ragged boy with close-cropped head, and trousers that had once belonged to an elder brother and, cut down and all, were still too big for him. The inexpert re-tailoring made him look as if one of his buttocks was twice the size of the other. He made hup-hup noises. He poked with an ash-twig at the animal's flank. He grandly ignored me; and I was too absorbed by the mystery of the cow that used the shop-door to think twice about the significance of that little cropped head. Clutching my fourpence and facing up to fate, I pushed open the door. The same bell rang to herald my entrance that had rung to tell of the departure of the cow.

Harry the Barber was saying: It's kinda awkward at times. You'd be amazed how some people are affected when she walks in one door and out the other. But the only other exit is to make her swim the river at the bottom of the yard.

—You've no back entrance, said one of the two customers.

He had two gold teeth and talked through his nose.

—Nor exit, said Harry.

—The town, said the second customer, isn't much of a place for a cow or a collie dog.

He was a mountainy farmer with a spade-shaped beard.

—Still she's as good as gold, Harry said. Here in the shop she never once transgressed.

—House trained you might say, said the man with the gold teeth.

—Nothing amiss with dung in its own place, said the farmer.

Harry's professional coat had once, but a long time ago, been white. He was shaving the man with the gold teeth and trimming the farmer, and he moved between them like a man who couldn't make up his mind which was which. Now and again he paused before a spotty mirror, and pulled and pushed at the mottled skin of his face and studied his bloodshot eyes. His hand was shaking very badly.

—It's a godsend, he said, to have your own cow when you have a lot of children.

A battered radio, fixed to the wall above the mirror, allowed a human voice, punctuated by atmospheric explosions, to sing about Genevieve, sweet Genevieve.

—The old girl's still threshing, said the man with the gold teeth. Last heard her name mentioned in Boston.

He made himself comfortable in the chair while Harry absented himself for a moment to snip at the farmer. He crossed his long legs. He had huge feet and shiny patent-leather boots which he surveyed with interest.

—It riles me, he said. Young folk around here have no enterprise. Market-day now, go-ahead young fellow could take a fortune out there on the High Street. As a shoeshine.

—He'd have to kneel down, said the farmer.

Quoting from a patriotic ballad I'd learned at school, in which a brave blacksmith refused to stoop to shoe the horse of a redcoat captain, Harry said: I kneel but to my God above, I ne'er will bow to you.

—People in this town, said the farmer, find it hard enough to kneel to the Creator that made them, let alone to clean another man's shoes. Towney pride.

—Pride never pockets dollars, said the man from Boston.

Inexplicably the volume of the radio rose like a tidal wave and the talk was drowned in one last despairing wail to Genevieve.

—Switch her off, said the Boston man. Get her outa here.

—More likely, said Harry as he evicted Genevieve, the mean mountainy farmers would spit on you or walk over you if you were misguided enough to kneel down to clean the cowdung off their boots.

—No harm in cowdung, said the farmer, in its proper place.

—Country's not organized, said Gold Teeth. No co-operation.

They went on like that while, unnoticed, I sat in trepidation and foreboding of the moment when the two would leave and I would be alone with, and at the mercy of, Harry.

The old farmer was the first to go. He stood up stiffly and Harry handed him a black bowler and a blackthorn stick. He wore nailed boots and leather leggings. When he took out a cloth purse to pay, as he put it, for the shearing, he turned his back on the company while he opened it and extracted the coins. But he gave me a penny as he passed and a pat on the head. The Boston man was better still. He mopped his face for a long time with a hot damp towel, and swayed like a feinting boxer before the mirror, and dried his face with another towel, and tossed a wide-brimmed straw hat in the air, and caught it on his head as it was descending, and shook hands with Harry and pretended to box him, and spun a half-crown at me, and shook my hand when I fielded it and was gone with a slam of the door that set the bell jangling for ages. Rich I was then beyond the dreams of avarice, but I needed it all as divine compensation for what was to follow.

—Kneel up on the chair, lad, said Harry, or my back will be broke stooping to you.

Brightly I began to recite: I kneel but to my God above . . .

—The cleverness of some people, said Harry. But kneel up all the same.

So up I knelt, my back to the mirror, my face to a wall papered with coloured illustrations of running horses, and Harry the High Priest robed me in a sacrificial cloth that like his coat of office had been white a long time ago. From faraway pastures the diminutive cowherd returned, ash twig in hand, and stood boldly staring at my misery; and only then, as I looked at the little round marble of a close-cropped head, and as the scissors began to snip around my ears, did I realize with sickening horror what was in store for me. Doomed I was to receive one of the first crew-cuts ever administered in our town—outside Harry's own family, that is, or the fever hospital where they cropped the heads of the scarlatina patients.

That negative hair-style has since then become for a while one of the fashionable things but, at that period and in that town, it was a disgrace and humiliation. To be balded was a rural disorder, to be an object of laughter like the country boys who came with their parents into the town for market-days and holidays of obligation. To be balded was an uncouth and backward way to be; and, to make things worse, once already in my life I had, through an excess of masculine vanity, brought that disgrace and humiliation on myself. The relentless scissors snipped. The hideous little herd eyed me. Swathed in off-white cerements I was powerless to escape. Behind tightly-shut eyelids I saw my aunt's long, thatched, white-washed farmhouse, ten miles from the town. Every summer I holidayed there. There was a great farmyard with barns, byres and stables, a deep orchard, and stepping-stones across the bog-red water of the burn that went down to join the Fairywater. There was a vile-tasting duck-pond that I once fell into, cherry trees that were regularly spoliated by the blackbirds and by barefooted boys passing the road to school; and my dowager of an Aunt Kate peering through spectacles on the tip of her nose at the eggs she polished for market.

There was also Cousin Patrick's enviable jungle of glossy, curling, black hair.

—Aunt Kate, my query would go, how can I make my hair curl like Patrick's?

She was a tall, aged, angular widow, clad in black bombazine with beads on the bosom; and buttoned boots; and skirts to her ankles. Polishing eggs and peering she would answer absently: Patrick was forever and always out in the rain. It was the rain made his hair curl.

So every shower, soft or heavy, that blew up that summer from the south-west, found me standing under it as patient as the stump of a bush. The wagtails, for whom the rain brought up the worms and the white grubs, picked and hopped around me like mechanical toys. I became their friend and familiar. The way to catch wagtails, I was told, was to put salt on their tails and then catch them, but that summer I felt that I could, without salt, have captured the full of an aviary. We were rain-worshippers together. But when, in the middle of a downpour that came to cool earth and air after thunder and lightning, I was found, soaked to the skin and standing under a sycamore to get the added hair-curling benefit of the drops from the sodden leaves, Aunt Kate altered her advice.

—Once, she said, Patrick had his hair cut very short and it was curly when it grew again.

She was too old and too gentle, and too interested in polishing eggs, to allow for the ruthless literalness and pure faith of childhood, or to foresee the self-shearing I was to do with her best scissors out behind the red-currant bushes in the most secluded corner of the orchard. The roars of laughter with which the servant-boys around the farm greeted me convinced me that a shorn head was a shameful thing, and that I had accepted too readily the casual words of a rambling old woman; and a balded head became forever the mark of a fool. But then it didn't matter so much in the country where bald-headed little boys were the fashion and where there was nobody of much importance to see you. By the time the holidays were over my luxuriant locks had almost grown again—as uncurled as ever.

But this was farandaway worse. The barber's baleful little son stared at me without speaking and then, unfeelingly, began to munch a crab-apple. Harry was a shaking, red-faced, savage Apache, and I knew I was being scalped. Between me and the shelter of home and my school-cap there were leagues of crowded streets where everybody knew me, and on the day after tomorrow, the fabulous city of Dublin where there was no such thing as a baldy boy, and where thousands of people would stop on the street to look and laugh at the wonder.

Like a terrified mouse I ran all the way home, taking no time even to buy sweets with my hoard of money. Only it would further have drawn attention to my nakedness I would have tried to hide my shaven crown with my hands. One corner-boy, perceiving my plight, called: Wee scaldy-bird, did you fall out of the nest?

The memory of featherless baby-birds, once seen in a nest, afflicted me with nausea.

—He cut you a bit close, my mother said placidly. But it'll grow again.

Putting on my school-cap firmly I went out to the garden at the back of the house and sat on a stone and just looked at the ground.

The journey was a glory. The world stayed there, swimming in sunshine, while I swept past like a king or an angel and inspected it from on high. It gave me my first vision of the Mountains of Pomeroy, as the song calls them, which aren't mountains at all but green, smooth, glacial hills; and the apple-orchards of Armagh; and the slow-flowing sullen River Bann; and the great valley around the town of Newry; and the Mountains of Mourne, which are real mountains, sweeping down to the sea as they do in another song; and the Irish Sea itself, asleep along the flat shores of Louth and Meath and North County Dublin, or creeping on hands and knees into estuaries and the harbours of little towns. I sucked hard sweets and kept my eyes to the window and didn't have to expose myself by taking off my head-covering. My father told me the name of everything, and once when a hapless fellow-townsman, who was travelling in the same carriage, made a fool of himself by mistaking the Mourne Mountains for the Hills of Donegal, my father silenced him with a genial glance and the words: Weak on topography, James.

—I never travelled like you, Tommy, the sad man said apologetically. I never saw Africa nor the Barbadoes.

Being at the age when a boy thinks his father knows everything—before he grows a little older and comes to think, with equal foolishness, that his father knows nothing—I was mightily pleased, and so was my father who prided himself on his knowledge of places.

So, two happy men, we came to the station at Dublin and

stepped out on to the interminable platform, and I took three steps and knew I was doomed. It was bad enough to be a leper, but it was torture out-and-out to have to carry a bell to draw public attention to your misfortune. Those three steps on the hard platform told me that, as fatally as any leper, I bore with me my self-accusing bell. It went clink-clink-clink. It was the iron tip on the heel of my left shoe. For days it had been threatening to come loose and jingle and this, in the sorry malevolence of things, was the moment it would choose. Clink, clink, clink. To me it was as audible as the clanking chains of an ancestral ghost. The irritating sound came up distinctly over the puffing and shunting of engines, the shouting of porters, the rattling of their barrows. It went to hell altogether as I hobbled, trying to be inconspicuous, down the marble steps to the street, and was still audible above the sound of trams and buses, motor-cars and four-wheeled horse-drays. To the furthest limits of the city I heard it proclaim the arrival of that wonder of wonders, the Celebrated Bald Boy who was ashamed to take off his cap. All around me moved thousands of smooth-spoken, elegantly-dressed, hatless, capless, velvet-footed people with heads of hair to be proud of. No city person would be barbarous enough to have iron tips on the heels of his or her boots or shoes. They didn't seem to notice me as I passed, but I imputed that to their excessive politeness. Behind unsmiling masks of faces they were really paralytic with mocking laughter. To look back I didn't dare in case I'd see somebody staring in hilarious wonder after my clinking retreat.

—The zoo I promised you, my father said. The zoo you must have. We'll have the convent afterwards for a change. You're rattling like all the hammers in Hamilton's smithy.

That recall to the homely image of the three good giants and their workshop fortified me for the walk to the restaurant for lunch. Keeping my eyes steadfastly down, and priding myself on coming from a land where giant men could swing hammers as city people couldn't, I resolved to see only the feet of the passing people and, after a while, I found myself repeating to myself, as if the words had magic and amusement in them: Feet, feet, feet, big feet, little feet, clean feet, dirty feet, and so on. For there were all sorts of feet in the world and, lacking feet, walking was not possible, and thinking of feet took my mind away from heads. The restaurant posed no new trials. Undisturbed, my heel didn't rattle. It was the day of a big hurling match and the place was full of red-faced countrymen who ate with their caps on. Their example was good enough for me and, eating my food, I told myself with heavenly glee that within an hour I would, for the first time in my life, see elephants and monkeys, lions, tigers, cobras, kangaroos, all the wonders of swamp, savannah and jungle.

But, alas, even my time in the zoo was torn and agonized by changing, conflicting emotions. Most of the caged animals, like the red-faced countrymen with their caps on, seemed to be my allies. There was a lot of baldness among them, particularly on the most unexpected parts of the monkeys. The brown orang-outang, swinging round and round on a pole and apparently content to do just that for the whole long day, didn't appear to be in the least worried by his bald patches. But was the pitiful, pacing restlessness of the spotted hyena the result of some clumsy jungle barber stumping his tail—possibly with snapping teeth? The long grey-white hair of the lazy, peaceful llama; and hair like a crown on the top of the hump of the white Arabian dromedary; the legs of the polar bear that were so hairy they made him look as if he were wearing white pyjamas far too big for him; the mane of the king of beasts that no drunken barber would ever defile—all these convinced me that hair was immortal and resilient and would, except in the case of the crowns of old men, grow again. But then the hairless, slinking creatures filled me with horror: pythons, crocodiles, alligators, terrapins, turtles, monitor lizards with forked darting tongues, even the enormous hippo wallowing in muddy water and turning his unmannerly tail-end to all visitors. The sea-lion was redeemed by his antics and his whiskers.

The lovely little hairy toy-ponies from Shetland pulled charabancs crowded with laughing children and clinked their harness bells so as to drown the noise of my loose heel-tip. Every time they swept past, my father said: Care for a jaunt, boy?

To the point of tears I refused, for my heart was bursting to board one of those charabancs. But how could I explain that I was afraid and ashamed in case some boisterous city boy among the passengers might knock off my cap and expose me to mockery?

A great eagle, motionless and alone in pride on a tree in a high-wired enclosure, looked as if he was even proud of his bald head. But other birds, I thought, leave him solitary up there just because he is bald; and his grim, stern, isolated image haunted me all across the city to the gate of the convent, the Nazareth House, where my cousin, Sister Barbara, was a nun and where my greatest agony was to begin. Looking, with my cap on me, at captive animals, was one thing. Being looked at, when my cap was off, was another and nuns and orphans are awful people for looking at you.

—Call everybody sister, said my father, except the reverend mother and, when I find out which of them she is, I'll give you a dig in the ribs. And take your cap off, I'm sorry to say, said he. We have to act like gentlemen and nuns are ladies.

He pressed the convent bell. The gate slowly opened and we looked into a whole cosmos of giggling girls in blue dresses and white bows and pigtails and shiny shoes. Oh my misfortune and unholy luck that it should have been playtime for all the little female orphans in the convent just when I arrived among them looking more like an orphan than any one of them. They didn't, I suppose, see many boys, and a bald-headed boy, his face purple with blushing, his cap in his hand, his heel-tip rattling, was just too good to be true. Looking back at it now I can, perhaps, admit that those little atomies of womanhood giggled every day and all the time, at playtime. But, at that moment, when the door-portress, all swinging rosary beads and flapping black tails, led us across the playground I felt that every giggle was meant for me, and I cursed Harry the Barber to places Dante never heard of and hoped that overnight his red cow with the crumpled horn would change into a slinking, odorous, odious hyena; or into a pacing tiger that would devour his cowherd of a son; or that all his customers would change into reptiles condemned to wander sleek and hairless to the judgement seat of God and beyond.

A door closed behind us. The giggles were no longer heard. We

followed the portress along a passage polished with such extrava-
gance that it must have cost many a visitor, or hapless convent
chaplain, a broken femur or radius. Into a parlour with a bare
polished table in the centre of the floor, twelve stiff chairs around,
and a portrait on the wall of a man that my father said was an
archbishop. Nobody, you were sure, had ever lived or laughed in
that room. The door closed behind the departing portress. The
archbishop frowned down at us.

—Your heel in the passage, said my father, would outsound the
convent bells.

With the shame burned into me by the giggles I hadn't for a
while heard the heel. I had been the fox who lost his brush, the
Chinese mandarin who lost his pigtail.

—Put your hoof on this chair here to see can I do anything about
it.

He pulled and hammered, and stopped pulling because he said
if the heeltip came the shoe would come with it and, possibly, the
foot as well. He was still hammering, hoping for the best, when the
door opened and six nuns entered, including the reverend mother;
and, bringing up the tail of the procession, two lay-sisters bearing
food for the two of us. What they saw was a perspiring middle-aged
man beating with the black bone-handle of the big claspknife with
which he cut his tobacco at the heel of the shoe of a bald little boy.

With what composure he could muster my father greeted them,
introduced his heir, and the two of us sat down to eat and the five
nuns and the reverend mother sat down in a semi-circle to look at
us. That's the way you eat when you go to a convent. This was the
zoo and my father and myself were the nut-cracking monkeys.
There was talk, too, of course, and Sister Barbara gave us each an
envelope full of holy medals and leaflets. But at no moment would I
have been surprised if reverend mother had tossed me a nut and,
obeying instinct, I had fielded, shelled and eaten it all in one
sweeping gesture, as but lately I had seen the black baboon do.

When the eating was over the reverend mother said: Now your
little boy, I feel sure, can sing.

She might also have said: Your little boy can, I feel sure, by the cut of him and the head of him, swing round a pole like the orang-outang.

The way it was I might as well have been singing as sitting there, so up I stood and breathed deeply and squared myself for action. If I had had hair on my head I wouldn't have lost my wits and would, like any Christian gentleman, have sung about Erin remembering the days of old ere her faithless sons betrayed her. As it was, with the strain and the shame, and with the naked soft top of my head exposed to the raging elements, I went mad and sang a song I had heard sung when the Hamiltons swung their mighty hammers above the burning iron.

—One Paddy Doyle, I told the nuns, lived in Killarney and he loved a maid named Betsy Toole.

It went on from bad to worse, but when my mortified parent made a move to stop me the reverend mother raised her hand and said: It was my father's favourite song—Doran's Ass.

—Now Paddy that day had taken liquor, I assured them, which made his spirits feel light and gay. Says he, the divil a bit use in walking quicker for I know she'll meet me on the way.

The shrill playing voices of the giggling girls were faraway as I related how drunken Paddy fell asleep in the ditch with Doran's jackass and embraced the animal in mistake for his true love. My voice was a bawdy bleat in the hollow, holy heart of eternity.

When the song had ended and I had modestly accepted the applause there was more talk and the lay-sisters brought in ice-cream. Then the reverend mother and Sister Barbara walked us across a playground now mercifully empty and bade farewell at the gate. The reverend mother put her hand into a slit in the side of her habit and went down and down until the better half of her arm vanished, then surfaced again with a box of chocolates in the hand. She gave it to me, and stooped and kissed the tonsured crown of my head.

—That song, she said, I haven't heard it in years.

—That I could easily believe, said my father as the gate closed behind us.

Then in awed tones he added: There's no doubt about it. Suffer the little children. Come on, son, and we'll see the laughing mirrors in the Fun Palace before we catch the rattler.

The box of chocolates shone like a sun.

—Haven't nuns, Da, I said, terrible deep trouser pockets?

So perturbed I was and yet, because of the chocolates, so over-joyed that I was in the tram on my way to the centre of the city before I realized I had left my cap in the convent parlour.

—Leave it be, said my father. They can have it as a relic of the man who told them about Paddy Doyle and Doran's ass. Their prayers and that kiss of peace will make your golden locks grow again as strong as corn stubble.

In the Fun Palace there were two girls in bathing-suits lying in cubes of ice to show they could do it, and a fat woman who weighed 40 stone and wore an outsize bathing-suit and who looked at me and slapped her thigh and laughed and said to my father: Ain't I a dainty little lass?

In this underground world the Celebrated Bald Boy could fade into his background and be a freak among freaks.

In a glass case a witch with a conical hat raised both hands when sixpence went into a slot and a printed slip telling your fortune came out of another slot. In another glass case a ghost, obligingly, and also for sixpence, entered a sombre panelled room and fright-ened a man in a four-poster bed so that he hid under the bed-clothes. The ghost, having done his sixpennyworth of haunting, vanished backways through a crack in the panelling.

Ardent queues lined up to peer into a small lighted glass box to share the butler's keyhole vision.

—It wouldn't interest us, my father said.

He steered me past the devotees and we paid our money and stepped into the hall of mirrors which, at first sight, might have been the hall of maniacs, because the six or seven people within were looking at the walls and doubling up and roaring with laugh-ter. So I turned and looked into the first mirror and saw my father, twelve feet long if he was an inch, and wriggling like the eel I once saw in semi-sunlight water under the arch of Donnelly's bridge on the Camowen river. Standing beside him, as I was, I was yet, in the most uncanny fashion, completely invisible; and in the second mirror my father was a little fat schoolboy and my bald head was a Shrove Tuesday pancake with currants for eyes; and in the third mirror my father was all head and no body and I was all legs topped by a head like a pine-cone. By the fourth mirror the tears of laughter were blinding me and, in blurred vision, I saw red-faced Harry shaking like an aspen leaf; and the man from Boston, all gold teeth, jumping and dancing and swinging from the farmer's beard; and the reverend mother with an arm a mile long pulling boxes of chocolates out of a bottomless pocket; and the red cow with floppy feet slithering and sitting down in Harry's shop and refusing to get up; and the giant Hamiltons, adopting all shapes and sizes, and confronted with hammers either so tiny as to be useless or too big and heavy to raise off the ground. The whole world I knew and the people in it were subject to comic mutation.

—Stop laughing, son, said my father at last, or we'll miss the train.

He wiped the tears from my eyes but he mightn't have bothered. They were as wet as ever before I got to the street. Every man and woman I looked at could have been cavorting before a comic, distorting mirror. There was something laughably odd about every one of them: big noses, red faces, legs too long or too short, behinds that waggled, clothes that didn't fit. Every one of them had a cow in the house. My bald head mattered no longer: it cut me off from no community. Let whoever liked laugh at me, I'd laugh back.

Tramping up the long platform I realized that a great silence had come around us. Engines snorted and shunted, trucks rattled, porters called each other names, newsboys sang their wares in sounds that weren't real words, fat women panicked and began to gallop in case the train might elude them. Yet, lacking one sound, it was all silence, and there was no clink-clink-clink, no warning note of my leper bell. Somewhere between the laughing mirrors and the station the iron tip had parted company with the heel and left me to walk as catfooted as an Aran islander or a wild Indian in pampooties, while it lay lost and neglected forever to be rolled over or walked on by the city's traffic. A part of me and of my town had died in exile and sorrow touched me for a while. Had I only detected the moment of our parting I could have preserved the heel-tip as a keepsake—warm in my trousers pocket.

But it was no evening for enduring sorrow. Before me lay the sights and thrills of the journey, and the reverend mother's chocolates, and the joys of telling and re-telling, and expanding for colour and poetry, my traveller's tales. In the school-room again when the shiny round ball that was the world was set spinning I knew I could follow it for more than 100 miles and tell my compeers that convents in the city were stuffed full of boxes of chocolates to reward brave boys who could sing; that, while China might be bursting with Chinamen, there were, in a house on the quays by the Liffey, mirrors that turned all men into objects of laughter; and that, while Harry the Barber might keep a cow in the house, it was little to what they kept closed in cages in the Phoenix Park in Dublin.

THE NIGHT WE RODE WITH SARSFIELD

THAT WAS THE house where I put the gooseberries back on the bushes by sticking them on the thorns. It wasn't one house but two houses under one roof, a thatched roof. Before I remember being there, I was there.

We came from the small village of Dromore to the big town of Omagh, the county town of Tyrone, in the spring of 1920, bad times in Ireland (Violence upon the roads/Violence of horses) particularly bad times in the north-east corner of Ulster. There have been any God's amount of bad times in the north-east corner of Ulster. There were no houses going in the big town and the nearest my father could find to his work was three miles away in the townland of Drumragh and under the one roof with Willy and Jinny Norris, a Presbyterian couple, brother and sister. They were small farmers.

That was the place then where I put the gooseberries back on the bushes by impaling them on the thorns. But not just yet because I wasn't twelve months old, a good age for a man and one of the best he's ever liable afterwards to experience: more care is taken of him, especially by women. No, the impaling of the gooseberries took place seven to eight years later. For, although we were only there six or so months until my father got a place in the town—in the last house in a laneway overlooking the green flowery banks of the serpentine Strule—we went on visiting Willy and Jinny until they died, and my father walked at their funeral and entered their church and knelt with the congregation: a thing that Roman Catholics were not by no means then supposed to do. Not knelt exactly but rested the hips on the seat and inclined the head: Ulster Presbyterians don't kneel, not even to God above.

It was a good lasting friendship with Willy and Jinny. There's an Irish proverb: *Nil aitheantas go haontigheas*. Or: You don't know anybody until you've lived in the one house with them.

Not one house, though, in this case but two houses under one roof which may be the next best thing.

Willy and Jinny had the one funeral because one night the house burned down—by accident. Nowadays when you say that a house or a shop or a pub or a factory burned down, it seems necessary to add—by accident. Although the neighbours, living next door in our house, did their best to rescue them and to save the whole structure with buckets of water from the spring-well which was down there surrounded by gooseberry bushes, they died, Willy from suffocation, Jinny from shock, the shock of the whole happening, the shock of loneliness at knowing that Willy was dead and that the long quiet evenings were over. However sadly and roughly they left the world, they went, I know, to a heaven of carefully-kept harvest fields, and Orange lilies in bloom on the lawn before the farmhouse, and trees heavy with fruit, and those long evenings spent spelling-out, by the combined light of oil-lamp and hearth fire, the contents of *The Christian Herald*. My three sisters who were all older than me said that that was the only literature, apart from the Bible, they had ever seen in the house but, at that time, that didn't mean much to me.

The place they lived in must have been the quietest place in the world. This was the way to get there.

The Cannonhill road went up from the town in three steps but those steps could only be taken by Titans. Halfways up the second step or steep hill there was on the right-hand side a tarred timber barn behind which such of the young as fancied, and some as didn't, used to box. My elder brother, there, chopped one of the town's bullies, who was a head-fighter, on the soft section of the crown of his head as he came charging like a bull, and that cured him of head-fighting for a long time. Every boy has an elder brother who can box.

The barn belonged to a farmer who would leave a team of horses standing in the field and go follow a brass band for the length of a day. Since the town had two brass bands, one military, one civilian, his sowing was always dilatory and his harvests very close to Christmas. He owned a butcher shop in the town but he had the word, Butcher, painted out and replaced by the word, Flesher, which some joker had told him was more modern and polite but which a lot of people thought wasn't exactly decent.

If you looked back from Cannonhill the prospect was really something: the whole town, spires and all, you could even see clear down into some of the streets; the winding river or rivers, the red brick of the county hospital on a hill across the valley, and beyond all that the mountains, Glenhordial where the water came from, Gortin Gap and Mullagharn and the high Sperrins. Sometime in the past, nobody knew when, there must have been a gun-emplacement on Cannonhill so as to give the place its name. Some of the local learned men talked vaguely about Oliver Cromwell but he was never next or near the place. There were, though, guns there in 1941 when a visit from the Germans seemed imminent and, indeed, they came near enough to bomb Belfast and Pennyburn in Derry City and were heard in the darkness over our town, and the whole population of Gallowshill, where I came from, took off for refuge up the three titanic steps of the Cannonhill road. It was a lovely June night, though, and everybody enjoyed themselves.

If any of those merry refugees had raced on beyond the ridge of Cannonhill they would have found themselves, Germans or no Germans, in the heart of quietness. The road goes down in easy curves through good farmland to the Drumragh River and the old graveyard where the gateway was closed with concrete and stone long before my time, and the dead sealed off forever. There's a sort of stile made out of protruding stones in the high wall and within—desolation, a fragment of a church wall that might be medieval, waist-high stagnant grass, table tombstones made anonymous by moss and lichen, a sinister hollow like a huge shellhole in the centre of the place where the dead, also anonymous, of the great famine of the 1840s were thrown coffinless, one on top of the other. A man who went to school with me used to call that hollow the navel of nothing and to explain in gruesome detail why and how the earth that once had been mounded had sunk into a hollow.

That same man ran away from home in 1938 to join the British navy. He survived the sinking of three destroyers on which he was a crew member: once, off the Faroes; once, for a change of temperature, in the Red Sea; and a third time at the Battle of Crete. It may be possible that the crew of the fourth destroyer he joined looked at him with some misgiving. A fellow townsman who had the misfortune to be in Crete as a groundsman with the RAF when the Germans were coming in low and dropping all sorts of unpleasant things to the great danger of life and limb, found a hole in the ground where he could rest unseen, and doing no harm to anybody, until he caught the next boat to Alexandria.

When he crawled into the hole who should be there but the thrice-torpedoed sailor reading *The Ulster Herald*. He said hello and went on reading. He was a cool one, and what I remember most about him is the infinite patience with which he helped me when, impelled by a passion for history, I decided to clean all the table tombstones in old Drumragh and recall from namelessness and oblivion the decent people who were buried there. It was a big project. Not surprisingly it was never completed, never even properly commenced, but it brought us one discovery: that one of the four people, all priests, buried under a stone that was flat to the ground and circled by giant yews, was a MacCathmhaoil (you could English it as Campbell or McCarvill) who had in history been known as the Sagart Costarnocht because he went about without boots or socks, and who in the penal days of proscribed Catholicism had said Mass in the open air at the Mass rock on Corra Duine mountain.

For that discovery our own parish priest praised us from the pulpit. He was a stern Irish republican who had been to the Irish college in Rome, had met D'Annunzio and approved of him and who always spoke of the Six Counties of north-east Ulster as *Hibernia Irredenta*. He was also, as became his calling, a stern Roman Catholic, and an antiquarian, and in honour of the past

and the shadow of the proscribed, barefooted priest, he had read
the Mass one Sunday at the rock on Corra Duine and watched, in
glory on the summit like the Lord himself, as the congregation
trooped in over the mountain from the seven separate parishes.

This ground is littered with things, cluttered with memories and
multiple associations. It turns out to be a long three miles from
Gallowshill to the house of Willy and Jinny Norris. With my
mother and my elder sisters I walked it so often, and later on with
friends and long after Willy and Jinny were gone and the house a
blackened ruin, the lawn a wilderness, the gooseberry bushes gone
to seed, the Orange lilies extinguished—miniature suns that would
never rise again in that place no more than life would ever come
back to the empty mansion of Johnny Pet Wilson. That was just to
the left before you turned into the Norris laneway, red-sanded, like
a tunnel with high hawthorn hedges and sycamores and ash trees
shining white and naked. My father had known Johnny Pet and
afterwards had woven mythologies about him: a big Presbyterian
farmer, the meanest and oddest man that had ever lived in those
parts. When his hired men, mostly Gaelic speakers from West
Donegal, once asked him for jam or treacle or syrup or, God help
us, butter itself, to moisten their dry bread, he said: Do you say
your prayers?
  —Yes, boss.
  They were puzzled.
  —Do you say the Lord's prayer?
  —Yes, boss.
  —Well, in the Lord's prayer it says: Give us this day our daily
bread. Damn the word about jam or treacle or syrup or butter.
  When he bought provisions in a shop in the town he specified:
So much of labouring man's bacon and so much of the good
bacon.
  For the hired men, the imported long-bottom American bacon.
For himself, the Limerick ham.
  He rose between four and five in the morning and expected his
men to be already out and about. He went around with an old

potato sack on his shoulders like a shawl, and followed always by a giant of a gentleman goat, stepping like a king's warhorse. The goat would attack you if you angered Johnny Pet, and when Johnny died the goat lay down and died on the same day. Their ghosts walked, it was well known, in the abandoned orchard where the apples had become half-crabs, through gaps in hedges and broken fences, and in the roofless rooms of the ruined house. Nobody had ever wanted to live there after the goat and Johnny Pet died. There were no relatives even to claim the hoarded fortune.

—If the goat had lived, my father said, he might have had the money and the place.

—The poor Donegals, my mother would say as she walked past Johnny Pet's ghost, and the ghost of the goat, on the way to see Willy and Jinny. Oh, the poor Donegals.

It was a phrase her mother had used when, from the doorstep of the farmhouse in which my mother was reared, the old lady would look west on a clear day and see the tip of the white cone of Mount Errigal, the Cock o' the North, 60 or more miles away, standing up and shining with shale over Gweedore and the Rosses of Donegal and by the edge of the open Atlantic. From that hard coast, a treeless place of diminutive fields fenced by drystone walls, of rocks, mountains, small lakes, empty moors and ocean winds the young Donegal people (both sexes) used to walk eastwards, sometimes barefoot, to hire out in the rich farms along the valley of the Strule, the Mourne and the Foyle—three fine names for different stages of the same river.

Or the young people, some of them hardly into their teens, might travel as far even as the potato fields of Fifeshire or Ayrshire. They'd stand in the streets at the hiring fairs to be eyed by the farmers, even by God to have their biceps tested to see what work was in them. The last of the hiring fairs I saw in Omagh in the early 1930s but by that time everybody was well dressed and wore boots and the institution, God be praised, was doomed. There was a big war on the way and the promise of work for all. But my mother, remembering the old days and thinking perhaps more of her own

mother than of the plight of the migratory labourers, would say:
The poor Donegals. Ah, the poor Donegals.

Then up the sheltered red-sanded boreen or laneway—the Gaelic
word would never at that time have been used by Ulster Presbyterians—to the glory of the Orange lilies and the trim land and in
the season, the trees heavy with fruit. Those gooseberries I particularly remember because one day when I raided the bushes more
than somewhat, to the fearful extent of a black-paper fourteen-
pound sugar-bag packed full, my sisters (elder) reproved me. In a
fit of remorse I began to stick the berries back on the thorns. Later
in life I found out that plucked fruit is plucked forever and that
berries do not grow on thorns.

Then another day the three sisters, two of them home on holidays from Dublin, said: Sing a song for Jinny and Willy.

Some children suffer a lot when adults ask them to sing or recite.
There's never really much asking about it. It's more a matter of get
up and show your paces and how clever you are, like a dancing dog
in a circus, or know the lash or the joys of going to bed supperless.
Or sometimes it's bribery: Sing up and you'll get this or that.

Once I remember—can I ever forget it?—the reverend mother of
a convent in Dublin gave me a box of chocolates because in the
presence of my mother and my cousin, who was a nun, and half the
community I brazenly sang:

> Paddy Doyle lived in Killarney
> And he loved a maid named Bessy Toole,
> Her tongue I know was tipped with blarney,
> But it seemed to him the golden rule.

But that was one of the exceptionally lucky days. I often wondered, too, where the reverend mother got the box of chocolates.
You didn't expect to find boxes of chocolates lying around convents in those austere days. She dived the depth of her right arm for
them into a sort of trousers-pocket in her habit, and the memory of
them and of the way I won them ever after braced me in vigour (as
the poet said) when asked to give a public performance.

—Up with you and sing, said the eldest sister.

Outside the sun shone. The lilies nodded and flashed like bronze. You could hear them. On a tailor's dummy, that Jinny had bought at an auction, Willy's bowler hat and sash were out airing for the Orange walk on the twelfth day in honour of King William and the battle of the Boyne. The sash was a lovely blue, a true blue, and the Orangemen who wore blue sashes were supposed to be teetotallers. Summer and all as it was the pyramid of peat was bright on the hearth and the kettle above it singing and swinging on the black crane, and Jinny's fresh scones were in three piles, one brown, one white, one spotted with currants and raisins, on the table and close to the coolness of the doorway.

—Sing up, said the second sister. Give us a bar.

—Nothing can stop him, said the third sister who was a cynic.

She was right. Or almost. Up I was and at it, with a song learned from another cousin, the nun's brother, who had been in 1920 in the IRA camp in the Sperrin mountains:

> We're off to Dublin in the green and the blue,
> Our helmets glitter in the sun,
> Our bayonets flash like lightning
> To the rattle of the Thompson gun.
> It's the dear old flag of Ireland, boys,
> That proudly waves on high,
> And the password of our order is:
> We'll conquer or we'll die.

The kettle sputtered and spat and boiled over. Jinny dived for it before the water could hit the ashes and raise a stink, or scald the backs of my legs where I stood shouting treason at Willy and the dummy in the bowler and the teetotaller's blue sash. It may have been a loyal Orange kettle. Willy was weeping with laughter and wiping the back of his left hand sideways across his eyes and his red moustache. In the confusion, the eldest sister, purple in the face with embarrassment, said: If you recited instead of singing. He's much better at reciting.

So I was—and proud of it. Off I went into a thundering galloping poem learned by heart from the *Our Boys*, a magazine that was nothing if not patriotic and was produced in Dublin by the Irish Christian Brothers.

> The night we rode with Sarsfield out from Limerick to meet
> The waggon-train that William hoped would help in our defeat
> How clearly I remember it though now my hair is white
> That clustered black and curly neath my trooper's cap that
>   night.

This time there was no stopping me. Anyway Willy wouldn't let them. He was enjoying himself. With the effrontery of one of those diabolical little children who have freak memories, even when they don't know what the words mean, I let them have the whole works, eight verses of eight lines each, right up to the big bang at Ballyneety on a Munster hillside at the high rock that is still called Sarsfield's Rock.

It is after the siege of Derry and the battle of the Boyne and the Jacobite disaster at the slope of Aughrim on the Galway road. The victorious Williamite armies gather round the remnants of the Jacobites locked up behind the walls of Limerick. The ammunition train, guns, and wagons of ball and powder, that will end the siege rumble on across the country. Then Sarsfield with the pick of his hard-riding men, and led by the Rapparee, Galloping Hogan, who knows every track and hillock and hollow and marsh and bush on the mountains of Silver Mine and Keeper and Slieve Felim, rides north by night and along the western bank of the big river:

> 'Twas silently we left the town and silently we rode,
> While o'er our heads the silent stars in silver beauty glowed.
> And silently and stealthily well led by one who knew,
> We crossed the shining Shannon at the ford of Killaloe.

On and on from one spur of the mountains to the next, then silently swooping down on the place where, within a day's drag from the city's battered walls, the well-guarded wagons rest for the night. For the joke of it the Williamite watchword is Sarsfield:

> The sleepy sentry on his rounds perhaps was musing o'er
> His happy days of childhood on the pleasant English shore,
> Perhaps was thinking of his home and wishing he were there
> When springtime makes the English land so wonderfully fair.
> At last our horses' hoofbeats and our jingling arms he heard.
> "Halt, who goes there?", the sentry cried. "Advance and give
>   the word."
> "The word is Sarsfield," cried our chief, "and stop us he who
>   can,
> "For Sarsfield is the word tonight and Sarsfield is the man."

Willy had stopped laughing, not with hostility but with excitement. This was a good story, well told. The wild riders ride with the horses' shoes back to front so that if a hostile scouting party should come on their tracks, the pursuit will be led the wrong way. The camp is captured. Below the rock a great hole is dug in the ground, the gun-powder sunk in it, the guns piled on the powder, the torch applied:

> We make a pile of captured guns and powder bags and stores,
> Then skyward in one flaming blast the great explosion roars.

All this is long long ago—even for the narrator in the poem. The hair is now grey that once clustered black and curly beneath his trooper's cap. Sarsfield, gallant Earl of Lucan, great captain of horsemen, is long dead on the plain of Landen or Neerwinden. Willy is silent, mourning all the past. Jinny by the table waits patiently to pour the tea:

> For I was one of Sarsfield's men though yet a boy in years
> I rode as one of Sarsfield's men and men were my compeers.
> They're dead the most of them, afar, yet they were Ireland's sons
> Who saved the walls of Limerick from the might of William's
>   guns.

No more than the sleepy sentry, my sisters never recovered from the shock. They still talk about it. As for myself, on my way home past the ghosts of Johnny Pet and the gentleman goat, I had a vague feeling that the reason why the poor girls were fussing so much was because the William that Sarsfield rode to defeat must have been Willy Norris himself. That was why the poem shouldn't be recited in his house, and fair play to him. But then why had Willy laughed so much? It was all very puzzling. Happy Ulster man that I then was I knew as little about politics and the ancient war of Orange and Green as I knew about the way gooseberries grew.

It wasn't until after my recital that they found out about the black-paper fourteen-pounder of a sugar-sack stuffed full of fruit. The manufacturers don't do sacks like that any more in this country. Not even paper like that any more. It was called crib-paper, because it was used, crumpled-up and worked-over and indented here and bulged out there to simulate the rock walls of the cave of Bethlehem in Christmas cribs.

For parcelling books I was looking for some of it in Dublin the other day, to be told that the only place I'd come up with it was some unlikely manufacturing town in Lancashire.

THE PLAYERS AND THE KINGS

THE TALL, MILD, bald Catholic curate crossed his long legs, wiped his pince-nez, and assured us that the play we were rehearsing was full of biblical lore. That was a mediocre form of encouragement, or consolation; because not the presence of King Herod, Gaspar, Melchior, Balthasar, nor of Annas the high priest, nor of the lovely spectre of the long-dead Mariamne, could make up for the play's one dreadful defect: there was no part in it for Harry the Pawn.

By legitimate descent, and by talent inherited from his father before him, Harry the Pawn was the town's chief comic. A play without the laughter that Harry could not help provoking was no play at all. Biblical lore might be all very well for gentle clergymen, Sunday sermons and fanatics. But do you remember the play in which Harry had been a horse-coper with a yellow muffler around his neck, and a yellow straw that he was chewing in the side of his mouth, and he making love to a servant girl that was seven feet high in a scarlet dress, telling her that she was as lovely as the pillar of fire that walked before Moses?

Or the play in which he had been a rascal of a poacher with a ferret in a box, or the other one in which he had been a journeyman house-painter with a Dublin accent you could cut with a knife?

In all those plays and parts he had been, quite simply, himself: the son of his father who was the best man ever to sing the song about the old grey mare. As in the case of his father the laughter began a few seconds before he stepped on the stage. Instinct told the people he was coming. There'd be electricity in the air in the town-hall theatre. It was hard with the laughter to hear what he was saying. But every little hop, skip and jump he made, every face he pulled, particularly behind the elongated back of the servant maid, registered as uproarious.

If, for a week afterwards, you came on three people laughing together on the Courthouse Hill or the High Street or in the Diamond before the church, you might know they were moved by the delights of memory. Some of the older people might even recall, tears in their eyes, the antics of a father who, straddled on a phantom grey mare, had long since moved off into the shadows, leaving to his son an inheritance of quicksilver.

—If there's laughter in heaven as well as joy, said Peter Quinlan, the schoolteacher, then that reclaimed sinner, Old Henry, and his grey mare would be the cause of it. But even in heaven, I'd say, they'd draw the line at biblical lore and no part for Harry the Pawn.

—Oh answer me, said Charles Edward Gogan the insurance agent.

He was at rehearsals in the musty decaying tottering parish hall: three old houses knocked, very awkwardly, into one. There was a poker school in every one of its lesser, dirty, gas-heated, gas-lighted rooms. But the eighth and largest room was sacred to the arts.

—Oh answer me, he intoned. Like rose leaves that enrich the dark brown earth, thy tremulous whispers will bedew my heart.

He was Herod and proud of it, because he loved to hear himself talk and Herod had most of the play to himself, torrents of fine words and two long-drawn-out fainting fits. He was asking an answer from the ghost of his murdered queen, Mariamne, who, out of understandable pique, stayed mute.

—In golden stars and zones and galaxies, said Napper Patterson, the draper who had once travelled for a season with a professional company.

He was Gamaliel, and this business of the star that guided the men from the east had set him off on astrology, which was quite in order, except that Napper, through misunderstanding or mispronunciation, made Gamaliel talk not of galaxies but of gallases, or suspenders, which he sold in his trade to keep the pants of the town in their proper places.

That was the style of the play. As you can see, it was a long ways away from horse-copers, journeymen with Dublin accents, and long servant girls in scarlet dresses.

Charles Edward Gogan was vain about some things: his fine singing and speaking voice, his Napoleonic stature and profile, his pigskin gloves lined with lambs' wool. He was never seen to wear the two gloves at the same time, but always to wear one and to carry the other. Stroking his impressive forehead with his gloveless hand he would say: Pause a moment. You're impinging on my sphere of thought.

Or sometimes it was: You're interrupting my train of thought.

When he was in one of those moods of infinite abstraction Napper Patterson said to him that no ancient and historic town was completely civilized if it hadn't its own set of players.

—As essential, Charles Edward, as the gasworks, or the drapery business. The costumes readymade for it in Harry the Pawn's army-and-navy stores.

With medals won in Africa or on Flanders' fields, and disposed of by old soldiers in days of penury, with swords and antique guns, and stuffed uniforms like watching men in the shadows, that store was more of a museum than a pawnshop.

—My train of thought exactly, Charles Edward said. But first to win over the Church.

So, bravely in step, they went to see the parish priest, Napper occasionally leaping from sidewalk to street, sidestepping and lunging to show how his old pro., leader of the travelling troupe, had taught him how to fight stage duels.

They sat in the pastor's brown leathery parlour, walled as solid as a fortress with theological tomes, and told him that a small section of the more intelligent young men of the town hoped to start a dramatic society to occupy pleasantly the long winter evenings in educative rehearsals, to keep other young men off the streets, out of pubs and card schools and, it was implied, off dark roads where they might be the ruin of young women. They mentioned tentatively Pope Pius XI, the Pope of Catholic Action.

The parish priest, grey, austere, unsmiling—no gentle curate had he ever been—sniffed snuff and listened.

They would like his approval and one of the curates as spiritual director.

He sneezed.

They pointed out that the proceeds would, naturally, go to decrease the debt on the church and the parish schools.

With the affability of the spider to the fly he said: What play were you thinking of making a start with?

Charles Edward had been to the university in Dublin. He acted once with the college players and once, at a theatre bar, had stood drinking beside, although he hadn't actually spoken to, the city's most notable dramatic critic. To people who never went to Dublin for longer than a fortnight at a stretch that contact amounted almost to celebrity and, because of it, Charles Edward's opinions on theatre were respected. At the committee meeting that sent Napper and himself out as ambassadors, everybody had agreed with his suggestion—with the exception of a sad reactionary who had mentioned the Colleen Bawn and Con the Shaughran and Arrah Na Pogue.

—My train of thought, said Charles Edward, has crashed. Poor William Yeats. Poor John M. Synge. Poor Augusta Lady Gregory. The world has changed in 50 years. Boucicault is dead and gone.

But in the presbytery parlour he could command no such withering sarcasm: the Abbey Theatre had suddenly no more significance than a horse-box; the college players and the noted critic were distant gesticulating puppets.

With a quiver in his voice he said: *The Plough and the Stars*, Father. O'Casey you know, Father.

The four last words had something of the awesome significance of the four last things. Napper Patterson looked earnestly out of the window, down the slope, over the trees, to humpy old roofs and sideways chimneys with smoky autumn dusk thickening around them—as if he expected to see there something nobody had ever seen before. Charles Edward studied his gloves. The parish priest looked into infinity. He said: I know only too well. The dirty dog. If that man wrote the Stations of the Cross you couldn't say them.

Memories of the college players and the critic and first nights at the Abbey came bravely, yet as wounded companions on a lost field, back to Charles Edward. He began: As Patrick Henry Pearse said of John Millington Synge . . .

He always gave every man his full name and hoped that the world would deal likewise with him.

—Pearse, the priest said. Didn't that man say that the grave of Wolfe Tone, a Protestant who cut his throat in jail, was a holier spot than the grave where St Patrick lies in Downpatrick? Didn't Synge write about James Lynchechaun, the murderous playboy of the western world, and disgrace us throughout the length and breadth of the United States of America?

—Not Exactly, Father.

—Not exactly? Sure God look to your wit, Charles Edward, son, and you running to school the day before yesterday, and short pants on you. Go ahead and start your playactors, and the blessing of the Almighty on the work. But let the plays you pick be uplifting plays or plays with a bit of decent fun in them. Father Gough will look after you. Good-night, now.

So they selected plays that would entertain the people without offending the parish priest and, for obvious box-office reasons, they went for decent fun rather than uplift.

That was where the horse-coper came in, straw in the corner of his mouth, to caper fore and aft of the scarlet servant; and the poacher with the ferret in the box; and the Dublin journeyman, and several other manifestations of Harry the Pawn. The soul of Charles Edward was in hell but our town-hall audiences were the gainers. They didn't give a twopenny ticket for Yeats, Synge, O'Casey or Shaw. They wanted and they got Harry, as funny with his black jowl on the stage, as he was on the street on a market-day selling old clothes to cautious farmers. He wore a pin-stripe, and a bowler on the back of his head; and his voice was good for 60 yards: Ladies and Gentlemen, I didn't come here to make my fortune. I've enough to last my lifetime—that is, if I die tonight. Gentlemen, a pair of pants that saw six harvests on the meanest farm on the mountains. Ladies, an elegant skirt, never lifted except in fun and, until recently, the property of a titled lady . . .

Then in the second month of the third season Father Gough, coming in sections out of the Baby Austin he drove with a knee high on each side of the wheel, stopped Charles Edward and myself on the street and told us of the idea. As a schoolboy with talent— meaning a loud voice, an examination knowledge of Shakespeare, an ability to read and memorize—I was involved in the idea to the extent of doubling as Annas the high priest (acts one and two) and one of the magi, the black one (acts three and four).

Father Gough had a friend who wrote mellifluous verse plays with echoes of Shakespeare, Shelley, Byron, Tennyson, Francis Thompson, Stephen Phillips and six or seven others. In one of his higher moments he let loose the full deluge of his verse to sweep the magi into our town on the first Sunday after the feast of the Epiphany. Sick and tired of comic horse-copers Charles Edward was ready for anything. This wasn't Shaw or Ibsen or even Claudel. It most certainly wasn't O'Casey. But it was verse of an order made to match the surge and thunder of Charles Edward's undeniably fine voice. So he assumed the king. As ruthless as any Herod he herded us, intoning the blankest of verse, before him. To this day sometimes in my dreams I go north with the Nile, the black king following the improbable star, sailing—as the verse said—for many evenings when the stream, the flaming mirror of a flaming sky, seemed lifeless, and I came to think myself the one thing living in a land long dead, till, black against a sky of blood and gold, some bird flapped by on lazy leaden wings.

At rehearsals only the sternest self-control kept my arms from becoming wings and bearing me away.

The lesser breeds who could speak no verse were kept busy making oriental costumes and furnishings out of the most unlikely materials. Butter boxes upended and covered with coloured paper became cushioned seats around the throne. Bowler hats, with cardboard crests glued on and the whole works covered in tinfoil, became Roman helmets. Frenzy of preparation seized everybody so violently that the ghost of Mariamne, Kitty Feeny who was a schoolmistress and who had no lines to speak, brought me twice a week to one of the smaller rooms in the parish hall. In the daytime absence of the poker players, she coached me in verse-speaking and stage movement. She elocuted. I echoed. She pushed me here and there until I was dazed with buffeting, drugged and breathing her perfume; and, although I was both a Jewish high priest and a black wise man from the Upper Nile, just a little puzzled as to what she was about.

But Harry the Pawn sulked and stayed away from rehearsals.

Peter Quinlan said: We can't leave him out. He'd never forgive us. The people would tear down the hall.

—We can't put him in, Charles Edward said. They'll laugh as soon as they see him. Laughter, think of it, in the halls of Herod.

—Couldn't we change it a bit, Napper Patterson said. My old pro. was always chopping and changing. Even Shakespeare. Put in a song or something. A porter in Herod's palace. Knock. Knock. Knock. Enter Gamaliel in haste.

—Do you want us all and Father Gough, to end up in Derry Jail? Shakespeare's dead, said Charles Edward sadly. A living poet has his rights. We're not poets.

—No, Napper said. Still, Paddy Mack, the postman's not bad. You remember the one he wrote when Alexander McClintock, a stranger from Portadown, got the job in the new powerhouse over the head of Peter Brady who was born and reared in this town? Or the one about the postman on the rural walk who had his shave every morning by the edge of a bogpool on Arvalee moor?

Then the Holy Ghost descended on Father Gough. He said: God be praised. Put Harry in as the Roman envoy to the court of Herod. A short part, a few words. He'll be on and off before they get time to laugh. No one can say he didn't appear in the play.

So it was done. Rehearsals went on, with Harry as envoy from Caesar to Herod. Lines were learned and rehearsed to the grievous affliction of the non-acting members of any family that included one of the players. A schoolfellow of mine, who was a minor member of the cast, and myself came close to ignominious expulsion for fencing with two ancient cavalry sabres brought from Harry's shop to form portion of the accoutrement of the Nubian eunuchs. Christmas passed and a cold sleety New Year's Day. The dress rehearsal was held on the day after Epiphany. Brazen trumpets heralded the approach of Caesar's envoy. The trumpets were, in fact, Jamesy Lever of the town band blowing a French horn and walking up the rickety stairs behind the stage. The envoy, radiant in tinfoil, spoke his sparse lines, performed his scanty Roman civilities, delivered to Herod a schools-examination certificate rolled up to resemble an ancient scroll. While Herod unrolled the certificate the envoy went out backwards and bowing. Jamesy Lever, sitting on the stairs with Kitty Feeny, blew a valedictory blast, and only then did Peter Quinlan notice that the Roman envoy was in his bare feet.

Peter had made for the magi and the rest of the cast, slaves and eunuchs excepted, sandals of cheap yellow leather. The father of Peter had been a cobbler, but Peter had been educated, sent to London to Horace Walpole's Strawberry Hill to be trained as a teacher, torn up by the roots from hacked benches, smells of waxend and liquid blacking, from awl and hammer, idly-gossiping customers, and all the true skills of cobbling. So the sewing of the sandals wasn't everything it might have been. Yet they were well calculated to dazzle the eyes of our audience looking across footlights into the palace of an eastern king. Their yellow glory would by contrast make a bare-footed envoy look conspicuous—and funny. A provocation to the people. Time was short, the leather supply was finished, and Peter had left Harry out of his calculations.

Peter was the yellow king. He said: Harry, use my sandals on Sunday. I'll throw them across backstage when I make my first exit.

—Them things. I'd be a sight more comfortable in my bare ones.

—Merciful God, Harry. You're supposed to be an envoy from Augustus Caesar. Not a cotter's son going to school over the bog at the back of Dooish mountain. You're not a slave. You're not a eunuch.

—No, thank the Lord. And many a decent man's son went to school at the back of the mountain and learned as much as they learn in London.

Peter with patience passed over that one.

—Take my sandals, all the same. You'd make a horse's collar of the whole thing, going on in your bare feet. Do you think a man could go all the way unshod from Rome to Jerusalem?

—I've only to walk from the dressing-room to the stage. Barring a wood splinter, I don't see what could happen to me.

—Look, Harry. Myself and the other two kings make our exit to the left. Then the trumpet sounds. You're right, waiting. I slip off the sandals, throw them over to you. With the noise of the trumpet nobody will hear a sound. You slip them on and make your entrance, looking respectable.

—Amen, said Father Gough. Fit company for kings.

On the Sunday night the three kings, black, yellow and red, presented their credentials to Herod, listened politely to his long speeches and, meditating on golden stars and zones and galaxies, made their exit. In the left wing I helped Peter Quinlan to unbuckle his sandals. Down at the bottom of the stairs Jamesy Lever blew his first blast. It throbbed in the stage timbers, rustled the curtains, unsettled the ancient plaster yellowing on the walls. A French horn is a resounding instrument and Jamesy was a man of notable lungs.

Peter threw one sandal. I threw another. With the tumult of Jamesy Lever nobody heard the sound of their landing. Nobody, not even Harry, saw where they landed for the right wing was as dark as the black hole of Calcutta. On his bare knees Harry crawled in circles, accumulating splinters, cursing sibilantly, richly, methodically. His pasteboard and tinfoil lorica, his crested bowler hat glimmered in the darkness. In the darkest corner the tall mild bald curate sat in motionless silent discomfort, hiding in the shadows rather than join in the search and risk embarrassing Harry by thus admitting that he had overheard such market-day language.

Harry found the sandals and pulled them on. A strap of cheap leather snapped like sewing thread. Soldier of pagan Rome he invoked things nearer home than the shades of Hector or Hercules. The priest of Christian Rome sat further back into the shadows. Then Harry was on his feet and striding across the threshold of Herod's palace. Hopefully the people, weary with long speeches, applauded. Unhappy in his panoply of cardboard and tinfoil, and in the thought that he was doomed to disappoint his adorers, he glanced nervously over the footlights, stepped on the loose end of the broken strap, and arrived on hands and knees before the throne of Herod, above him a Nubian eunuch holding an ancient cavalry sabre.

Charles Edward did his best. He grasped the school certificate, raised his hand and the certificate in what he would have called a regal gesture. He gagged:

Rise, Roman envoy, rise, nor have it said
That Roman knee was hooked at Herod's throne.

But Harry the Pawn's people were on their feet, all the cloying, unintelligible blank verse forgotten in the ecstasy of the fun that only Harry could inspire. The merit—undeniable—of Charles Edward's impromptu composition, even the last roars of Jamesy Lever's horn were lost in the cheering, laughing, whistling, hand-clapping, foot-stamping appreciation.

One voice called: Who goes there?

Another voice answered: Harry from the pawnshop on his old grey mare.

At the back of the hall twenty boys from Stream Hill began to chant: Hear, hear, Harry's here.

The whole hall, apart from the swanky people in the front rows of seats, took up the chorus: What the hell do we care now?

Louder and louder, as the heavy moth-eaten curtain descended like the centuries cutting off Herod's Jerusalem from our town as Harry the Pawn had fashioned it.

Until order was, in a sort of a way, restored by the gentle pleading of Father Gough.

There were funnier things in the play but nobody noticed them. St Joseph in the last act forgot altogether about his white beard and when, too late, he realised his nakedness, he panicked and mispronounced every long word in the seventeen lines he had to say. A Nubian eunuch presenting, at Herod's command, a seat to Annas, turned up a coloured-paper-covered butter box so far that the naked wood and the legend printed on it—Shaneragh Creamery. Twenty-eight Pounds—were visible halfways down the hall.

But the decent men who played the parts of St Joseph and that Nubian eunuch weren't natural-born comics, and Harry the Pawn was; and Harry sat in the dressing-room with his head in his hands, ashamed, for the first time in his life, of the fun that followed him, saying again and again: They'll never take me seriously. Boys, I disgraced myself and I disgraced the players.

Every time he said that, Peter Quinlan answered him and said: My fault, Harry, and those sandals.

Until Harry shouted: Now listen to me, Peter. You wouldn't, would you, expect an envoy from Augustus Caesar to come from Rome to Jerusalem on his bare feet?

On the dark streets as I walked home groups of contented people were saying: That Harry's a good one. Like his father before him. He'd split the sides of a carthorse. Or the old grey mare, herself. He'd put life into anything.

I was the black king and I had forgotten to take the grease off my face. The Court-house clock struck midnight. My cheeks were tight and stiff and there was an oily taste in my mouth. Through the dark dying streets I sailed for many evenings when the stream, the flaming mirror of a flaming sky seemed lifeless, and I came to think myself the one thing living in a land long dead.

In the hallway of Kitty Feeny's lodgings, Kitty and Jamesy Lever were grappled like catch-as-catch-can wrestlers. The French horn, wearing a white coat, was on the ground beside them.

Some bird flapped by on lazy leaden wings.

The sound of kissing was distinct and succulent, and too late I knew the benefits of elocution and stage movement.

> Like rose leaves that enrich the dark brown earth.
> Thy tremulous whispers.
> Oh, answer me.

THE FAIRY WOMEN OF LISBELLAW

IF IT HADN'T been for an elderly blonde that I saw sitting in the sun in a bikini on a lawn in Atlanta, Georgia, I'd never have remembered him again. She was a good 40 paces away from me as I stepped out with two friends from the door of my yellow-brick apartment building. Her back was towards us. She was the only object that disturbed the green grass, and very green it was to grow up out of the red clay of the dry sunny south.

She swivelled her head, left to right, and looked around at us. Although I didn't know who she was and had never even seen her before or, at any rate, had never seen that much of her, I waved my right hand. For beyond her, although in reality there was nothing but the street called Ponce de Leon where it ceases to be suburbia and becomes a stretch of rooming-houses and heavy traffic, and black girls washing cars, and a good Greek restaurant on the far side of the traffic, I saw clearly the Atlantic rolling in on the cliffs of Donegal, and the dark rocks of Roguey under which only the most courageous ever venture to swim.

So Gene asked me who the blonde on the grass was and I said I didn't know.

—But you waved at her.

—Wouldn't you wave at any girl in a bikini?

—A girl, Dolores said.

—I waved at the past.

—You sure did, Gene said. She's 90. You crazy Irish.

—We're a friendly people, I said.

We walked away from the aged blonde towards the car-park at the back of the apartments.

I gave up trying to be a Jesuit in the second year of the novitiate, not because my vocation, as we called it, had weakened—I gravely

doubt if I'd ever heard a voice calling me anywhere—but because I
had a broken back. Well, it wasn't exactly broken the way you'd
snap a twig. It was a spinal lesion, an injured spot on which the
bacillus that lurks in all of us settled to make it difficult for me to
bend if I was straight or to straighten up if I was bent, and to make
me feel that some unseen demon stabbed now and again, slowly
and carefully, with a thin red-hot knitting-needle about the region
of the third lumbar lump. Eighteen months of Christian patience it
took to exorcise that demon.

The Atlantic breakers, white and blue and green, and flashing a lot
of colours I could put no name to, came trampling and tumbling
up Bundoran strand. The surf was crowded with happy shouting
bathers. Little children, grave with excitement, rode slowly on tiny
brown hairy donkeys, and one enterprising entertainer had even
introduced a baby elephant. The hurdy-gurdy at the hobby-horses
and chairaplanes was squeezing the last drop of melody out of the
tune that went to the words about the old rustic bridge by the mill:

> 'Twas oftimes, dear Maggie, when years passed away,
> And we plighted lovers became . . .

The town was a long thin line along the coast behind me as I left
the red strand and climbed the steep short-grassed slope to the top
of the cliffs above Roguey Rocks. Golfers, like jerky clockwork toys,
moved, bent with no pain, drove with the intensity of cyclones, on
the windy links around Bundoran's grandest hotel. That wind was
strong and salty. Behind the town the flat-topped mountains, all
the way from Rossinver Braes to bare Ben Bulben, lay like sleeping
purple animals. The straps that held my back-splint in place were
cutting into my armpits and crotch. My shiny black jacket, that
had fitted well enough when I went into the hospital eighteen
months previously, had a hard job now to keep buttoned because
of the back-splint and a slight stomach spread developed in hospital. In that place of rolling ocean and salt shouting wind, purple
mountains, hurdy-gurdies and near-naked bathers, I was, and felt
I was, a cheerless sombre figure.

This clifftop walk was my path of escape. It brought me away from the happy all-together crowds that seemed so nastily to emphasize my own isolated predicament. Beyond Roguey the cliffs—flung spray rising high above them, high as they were, and spattering the rocks—swung directly eastwards and so, unavoidably did the path. It brought me by the bowl-shaped fresh-water spring, clear as crystal against solid rock, that was one of the wonders of those cliffs. It brought me by an even more wonderful wonder, the Fairy Bridges, where the sea had moled its way through weaknesses in the dark rock and, far back from the dangerous slanting edge of the cliffs, you could look down into deep terrifying cauldrons of boiling froth. Tragedies were always happening there: daring young people clambering down the sides of the cauldrons, to what purpose God alone knew, and losing foothold or handhold, and falling down where not all the lifeguards in the world could be of the least assistance to them.

Beyond those fatal Fairy Bridges the holiday crowd had vanished. There was an odd courting couple, snug from the wind behind a fence of green sods or a drystone wall, grazing nimble goats who sometimes attacked people; and inland, protected from the cliffs by walls and fences, easy grazing cattle. The great flat mountains were still visible, but the eye and imagination were taken now by the long rising-and-falling range of highlands far across the bay.

Poems had been written about this place: that vision of highlands, strand and sea, and far away the estuary of the River Erne. The strand was perilous with quicksands and so generally deserted.

> From Dooran to the Fairy Bridge
> And down by Tullan Strand,
> Level and long and white with waves,
> Where gull and curlew stand . . .

The wooden shelter that I sat and read in was as near to being my own exclusive property as made no difference. It was roofed with red tiles, and had no sides, and a cruciform wooden partition held up the roof and divided the structure into four parts so that no matter from what airt the wind did blow, myself and my book always had shelter. There I sat reading, day-dreaming, I was nineteen, remembering. Remembering now and again the Jesuit novitiate where, inexplicably, I had been happy in a brief fit of religious frenzy that was to be my ration ever since. A classical rectangular house that had once belonged to a great lord and, with red carpet on the main avenue, given welcome to an English king, sheltered in deep pine woods in the sleepy Irish midlands. Bells divided the holy day. Black-gowned neophytes made their meditations, walked modestly, talked circumspectly. Wood pigeons cooed continuously, and there were more bluebells and daffodils and red squirrels in those woods than I have ever seen anywhere else in the world.

But, to be honest, I was never quite sure what I was doing there and, if I was happy, it was happiness in a sort of trance that I felt uneasily must have its end. My lumbar spine made up my mind for me, and eighteen months surrounded by fresh and pleasant young Irish nurses convinced me that there were certain things that Jesuits were not normally supposed to have. So that my memories in the cruciform shelter were less about the Ignatian spiritual exercises than about dreams of fair women in blue-and-white uniforms. They were all there, around the corner by Ben Bulben and off through Sligo on the high road to Dublin. To the rocks and the seawind I repeated the names of the seven or eight of them I had fallen in love with: Lane, Devlin, Brady, Love, Callaghan, Mullarkey, O'Shea, Rush and Moynihan. On a recount: nine.

Far away a black-sailed boat that seemed scarcely to be moving came down the sand-channel of the Erne estuary to the sea. In the privacy of the shelter I eased the crotch-straps of the back-splint. It was made of good leather stretched on a light steel frame, it travelled from the neck to the buttocks, it smelled of horse-harness.

—Head out to sea, I said, when on your lee the breakers you

discern. Adieu to all the billowy coasts and the winding banks of Erne.

The tide, the bathers, the children, the donkeys, and even the baby elephant, had withdrawn for a while from the red half-moon of Bundoran Strand. Far out the frustrated breakers were less boisterous. The hurdy-gurdy was silent and the hobby-horses resting at their stalls, and in hotels and boarding-houses the evening meal was being demolished. In Miss Kerrigan's old-fashioned whitewashed Lios na Mara, or the Fort, God help us, by the sea, my mother looked up from her ham salad to say that I was late as usual.

—Sara Alice, leave him be, Miss Kerrigan said. He's thinking long. Waiting for the happy day when he gets back to his studies. Looking forward to his ordination, God bless him, the holy oil, the power to bind and loose.

Listening to her I kept my thoughts fixed on red squirrels flashing in bluebell woods, on the wasps' nest at the foot of the Spanish chestnut tree close to the croquet court, on the dark silent file of neophytes, eyes cast down, obeying the holy bell and walking to the chapel to morning oblation—along cold corridors and down a stairway up which unholy royalty had once staggered to bed. For I felt if my thoughts were on laughing young nurses, Lane, Devlin, Brady, Love, Callaghan, Mullarkey, O'Shea, Rush and Moynihan, my nine blue-and-white Muses, Miss Kerrigan's sharp brown eyes would discover those thoughts and betray the old Adam hiding behind the shiny black suit.

—Thinking long, she said again.

She was very fond of me and I wouldn't have hurt her for the world. Lios na Mara, too, was a place that caught the fancy as the average seaside boarding-house most certainly did not. It stood well back from the town's one interminable street, under a stone archway, secure and secluded in a grassy courtyard that overlooked the toy harbour where the fishing-boats and the seagulls were. It wasn't New York or Liverpool but it was the first harbour I ever saw and, as a child, I had actually thought that ships might sail from that harbour to anywhere or Antananarivo.

—This, said Miss Kerrigan, is Master McAtavey.

He had come into the room silently while, with my back to the door, I was fumbling with a napkin and sitting down to attack my ham. It was a surprise to find anyone except my mother and Miss Kerrigan who were girlhood friends, and myself, of course, by right of inheritance, in that small private parlour. The other guests ate elsewhere and did not presume.

—My only sister's son, said Miss Kerrigan.

—From the Glen of Glenties, said my mother who was hell all out for geography.

He was still standing, very tall and awkward, three paces away from the table.

—Sit down, Eunan dear, said my mother. Don't be shy.

She disliked shy people. She suspected them of dishonesty.

—He teaches school, said Miss Kerrigan.

—In the Vale of Dibbin, said my mother. A heavenly place. You know it, she said to me.

Then he blushed. Never before or since have I seen a blush like it. He had fair curly hair that was cropped too short and his eyes were a startlingly bright and childish blue. His navy-blue pinstripe was too short in the sleeves and, above strong square hands, the knobs on his wrists were as large as golfballs. He had taken two paces forward abruptly as if he were a sentry under command, towards his provender, so that the lower half of him was hidden by the table and I couldn't see whether the legs of his pants, like his sleeves, were too short. Not that I, with my shiny coat of clerical black straining to meet around my back-splint, was in any position to criticize. His blond skin—once it must have been blond—was so beaten by the heathery wind of the Glen of Glenties, and burned by the same sun that shines both on Glenties and Georgia, that even experts on the matter would have considered it quite impossible for him to blush.

But he did. The blush went upwards in little leaps or spurts, an inch or so at a time, from the tight white collar that squeezed his long neck, up and up, spreading, intensifying until his whole face shone, as the man said about the sunset, like a forge. He was a very shy master and let me say, to my credit, that I leaped up, offered him a chair, seated him at his ham salad, sat down again and talked non-stop for half an hour about the Vale of Dibbin and the Glen of Glenties. He choked over his ham, and played back to me the occasional yes or no, and I wasn't sure whether he was grateful or resentful. But I didn't care much, for I did know the places I talked about and to talk about them was a pleasure in itself.

The town of Glenties, I told them, was always bright with paint and so spotlessly clean that a scrap of paper or cigarette butt wasn't to be seen on the street, and a bluebottle fly, invading from some less-regulated town, wouldn't last for five minutes. A few miles away, the sands, under clear water where the Gweebarra River turned salt, shone like silver. In the Vale of Dibbin the neat white-washed farmhouses stood along the breast of the mountain and the clean fields sloped steeply down to a trout stream, all white cataracts and deep populated pools. On which river I had fished with my brother and a fat man called Joe Maguire who had fought at the Dardanelles and who wore a bowler hat even when he was fishing.

The life and times of Joe Maguire could have kept me going for half a day, but time was passing and I prized the private hours ahead when I would sit in my room and read and look down on the harbour and across the water at the happy company on the strand. They couldn't see me but I could see them and that, in some way or other, helped my morale. When I stopped to draw breath and chew ham I was glad to see that his blush had faded.

Miss Kerrigan listened, and watched me with loving brown eyes that were set deeply in a long wrinkled yellow face. She continuously rubbed her feet on the floor in a nervous way she had. That nervousness increased when she went to whist-drives and it was said that once, when she was running hard for first prize, she had rubbed a hole in the uncarpeted floor of the cardroom in a parish hall in a neighbouring town. She always dressed in black, in mourning for her father and mother who had died within the one week 30 years ago, and she was six feet two inches in height.

—What a memory, she said.

—A powerful man to tell stories, said my mother, like his father before him.

—A blessed gift, Miss Kerrigan said, and will stand to him well after ordination.

She must have meant something else, for no one could have suspected Miss Kerrigan of anti-clericalism.

—In the pulpit I mean, she said.

That didn't make it any better.

—I'll go for a walk now, said Eunan McAtavey.

Those were the first words I'd heard him say. They began as a whispering squeak and then spread out like a shout. They had clearly cost him premeditation and effort. He stood up. He didn't overturn his chair. He did drop his napkin. I picked it up for him.

—Bernard will go with you, Miss Kerrigan said.

—Bernard, my mother said, Eunan was never here before. He doesn't know his way around.

There went my private hours, but politeness compelled me and, at any rate, the ladies had me trapped.

Three lovely old ladies lived in that block of yellow-brick apartments. Taken all-together they were a sort of sign that something remained in a place where everything was rapidly changing.

They lived in a world of their own and had memories that had nothing whatsoever to do with the neighbours. Forty years ago, when they had come to live there, those apartments had been new and quite the thing. But suburbia in automobiles had swept far beyond them. The district decayed. The old ladies stayed on because they were too old, perhaps too poor, to move. Their neighbours now were myself, and the withered blonde whoever she was, and rowdy students who had lively parties and were occasionally evicted because the landlord would find six living in an apartment he had rented to two. To evict one such group his workmen had to take the door off the hinges. A few decent quiet linotype men lived there. The paper they had worked for in a more southern city had folded and they had come north to Atlanta to find work. A flock of go-go girls who were working down the street stayed for a while, brightened the lawn with bodies more naked than had ever startled Eunan McAtavey on Bundoran Strand, then flew off elsewhere. Their place was taken one evening by a fat oily bald man. From their windows the students made offensive noises. Two burglars who lived in another part of the city rented one of the yellow apartments to keep their loot in. The police came and were a whole afternoon carrying out and counting miscellaneous objects. My next-door neighbour was a girl from Nashville who was married at fifteen and whose husband dressed up as the tiger in the tank at a filling-station. He walked out every morning in his costume, his own head showing, the tiger's head grinning in his hand.

Gene drove down the slope. We passed the hotel where the black girl, coming to fill her fifth date for the night, had changed her mind and tried to steal the cash register instead, and had been shot dead by the night porter. We passed three liquor stores, an army induction centre, a Sears Roebuck, a waste-patch that had once been a ball-park and would, any day henceforth, sprout skyscrapers. The twenty black girls washing cars were, to keep cool, squirting water over each other. We passed a Yarab shrine, a Presbyterian centre, a motel, three churches, a pop place painted all purple, saloons, and shops, and one skyscraper hotel at the corner of Peachtree Street. Dolores was on the way to a suburban shopping centre to buy shoes.

That was the first of seven walks, dull enough, silence mostly between us, our chief activities just walking, or tossing driftwood back into the tide, or simply sitting and gazing out to sea. He couldn't swim and I because of my third lumbar lump and my back-splint, wasn't allowed to. Now and again, to break the silence, I played courier and pointed out the estuary, named the mountains and quoted the poetry. He showed no interest. He would walk stolidly beside me, and I had a crazy feeling that his arms swung together, both before him at the same time, both behind him at the same time, if you know what I mean. The pinstripe trousers were, indeed, too short, and the feet were considerable. When he put away the pinstripe—he said it was his Sunday-best and that the salt air faded dark cloth—and put on grey flannels with a dangerous crease, they also were too short. His oatmeal tweed jacket creaked from the shop and my back-splint answered. We were a fine pair to be seen on any gay promenade. He never nonchalantly put his hands in his pockets. When he stood up they hung by his side as if he had no control over them.

On the fifth walk I talked about the Jesuits and the novitiate and the weedy lake where boating and bathing were allowed, depending on the weather, on major Christian festivals. He responded by telling me, in broken spurts and mumbles, how he had spent two years of hell in a teachers' training college in Dublin, and that he might as well, for all the college ever taught him about life, have been incarcerated, he used that word, in Mountjoy Jail. That reference to life should have warned me.

On the sixth walk I mentioned the nurses and litanied the nine magic names and, growing reckless with wishful thinking, hinted at nights of love under dimmed lights. On the seventh walk he stopped in the sunshine, on a path through the dunes beyond Tullan Strand, and raised his stiff right arm to indicate the curves and hollows of the dry sand, the sleek comfort of the bent grass, and said hoarsely: This would be a bloody great place to have a woman.

—True enough, I said and felt guilty before his awkward innocent passion.

For by day in the shelter when the crotch straps were eased, by night in bed when my black garments were laid aside, I had skipped in fantasy up and down those same dunes, a satyr in pursuit of nine nymphs, or lurked in grassy corners to cut off unclad stragglers.

—The way you talk about the place I come from, he said, you'd think it was Blackpool or the Land of Youth.

It took me until the following day to appreciate that juxtaposition but, on reflection in the quietude of my room, it seemed reasonable. The poets don't tell us, but there must have been beaches and bathing beauties in the land to which Niamh led Oisin. Eunan, clearly, had given the matter long thought.

—It's lovely country, I said. A home for poets. The fishing's good.

—I don't fish. The only poetry I ever learned off by heart was this.

He stood up stiff as a guardsman, filled his lungs with seawind and let fly: Bracing breezes, silvery sands, booming breakers, lovely lands. Come to Bundoran.

It didn't occur to me, I remember, to be surprised at this display of eloquence. Being talkative myself, I must have assumed that there was as much talk in everyone, that it was welling up in him and that some day the dam would burst.

—I learned that out of an advertisement in the newspaper because it was my intention to come here to Bundoran for the women. I'd heard time and again that the place was hoaching with them during the Scottish holiday season.

Hoaching was a word we used to describe the way fingerling fish, in low water and warm weather, would swarm together at the mouths of pools. It was an evocative sultry word.

—What's holding you up? I said. They're everywhere to be seen.

Even in the lonely dunes that was true. Couples sprawled in sheltered corners. When they couldn't be seen they could be heard: muffled voices, and shrills of laughter quickly stifled, to remind the horseman passing by that love was all. The path we followed skirted the barbed wire of a military camp, went down a slope past an ancient churchyard to join the main road to Ballyshannon, Enniskillen, Omagh and Donegal town. Four green soldiers stood where the path joined the roadway and bantered and jackacted with six girls with bright flaring skirts and Glasgow accents.

—A surplus of two, he said. The soldiers have all the luck. You were lucky, too, with all those nurses. You struck it lucky. All good things. They say the nurses are the best. They know everything.

If I had not already come close to believing that my own

imaginings were reality I might have had an attack of conscience for all the tall tales I had told him.

—My trouble, Bernard, is that I can't talk to women. Even your mother and Miss Kerrigan frighten me. I never had the training. Where would I get it? With mountainy women as wild as the mountain sheep? Hands on them as hard as flagstones. I never got a bloody chance. Even in Dublin. The priests in the college wouldn't let you see daylight. The Vincentians.

—No, I said, I suppose the Vincentians wouldn't be so good at that. It wouldn't be on the curriculum.

It worried me a little that he didn't laugh at the idea. He looked straight in front of him. His mouth, and it was a small tight one for such a large man, was tightly closed—now that his talking was over for the moment. Muscle stood out on the point of his left jaw as if he had his teeth clenched on his grievance. The hard sidewalk, crowded with women, I suppose there must have been men there too, was hot under our feet, the long town ahead. He had touchingly used my name for the first time and so made me his ally, his sworn brother sweet, his voice when it came to putting chat on the women.

He was so awkward on his feet that he came into the class of men who can be described as getting in their own way. Walking beside him had all sorts of problems. It wasn't so bad when he was silent, as he seldom was after he had confessed to me his true reason for coming to Bundoran. For when he was silent he could follow a straight course as well as any man. But when he talked he moved, inch by inch as his blush did, sideways in little spurts towards his listener, and to emphasize his point he jabbed with his elbows. Or they did the jabbing all on their own, for of all the men I've ever known, he had the least control over his hands and elbows and feet. To make his feet more noticeable he purchased and wore a pair of those rubber-and-corduroy pampooties known to the civilized world as brothel creepers. They didn't go with the iron crease of his grey flannels nor the creaking jacket of honest oatmeal tweed. They were also too big for him, although that seemed impossible, but the toes certainly flopped when he walked or stumbled along sideways, elbowing, so that every 50 yards or so I had to dodge to the other side of him to save myself from bruises and correct our course. We were the rarest-looking pair of Romeos that ever walked out to rummage and ruin the girls, Scottish or Irish, that hoached in that summery pool.

—You're a man of the world, he said. You can talk to people.

Nobody had ever said that to me before. Nobody has ever said it since, although two months later, as a student in Dublin walking home by night, I picked up a little girl with a blue beret and a brown belted coat and protruding teeth, and kissed her good-night at her garden gate. She breathed deeply. She said: Boy, you've got technique.

Afterwards the risks I took with more sophisticated college lasses, to establish my claim to a technique of which until then I had been quite innocent, must have earned me an odd sort of reputation. But breathing bracing breezes, walking silvery sands, listening to, because I was unable to plunge into, booming breakers, it was up to me, as a man of the world, to do something for my hapless mountainy man. It wasn't going to be easy.

—Not that one, Bernard. She's as bold as brass by the cut of her.

—Isn't that what we're after, Eunan?

—She would talk the ass out of a pot. And the laughs of her.

The plump girl in orange swimsuit and blue bathing-cap ran, leaping and laughing, into the surf. Her thin blonde companion, in red suit and no cap, trotted demurely behind her, squeaking a little now and again. Little did the plump girl know how close she had come to the arms of Eunan McAtavey. He looked after her for a long time. He fancied her but he was afraid of her laughter.

—Not that one, Bernard, You couldn't get near her for lipstick.

This was a tall redhead, long flying red hair, who went round and round riding sidesaddle and flashing thighs on the hobby-horses. Her crimson mouth was, indeed, a size larger than nature, but only a man who had more on hand than he could deal with, would have faulted her for that. For a man who had nothing at all, nor ever had, Eunan of the Glen was mighty choosey. He feared laughter. He feared lipstick. He didn't want to spend money.

—Not that one, Bernard. She's a chain-smoker. Look at the butts on the ground around her. A bank manager couldn't keep her in cigarettes.

The thin girl in dark slacks and dark woollen sweater sat on a bench outside the Hamilton Hotel and blew out smoke as if she meant to blind the passers-by. She was gone beyond her first bloom but there was something appealingly wistful, and promising, about her dark steady eyes, and cheeks that hollowed as she sucked smoke.

—Not that pair, Bernard. They remind me of the mountainy girls at home.

They were sisters, two country girls, bright red berets, damp tails of hair straggling out from under the berets, belted fawn raincoats. Like ourselves and a hundred others, they had raced for shelter from an Atlantic squall to play the machines in hurdy-gurdy country. They stamped with delight in the deep churned discoloured sand. For fun, they shouldered each other like county footballers while they both grabbed for the one arm of the one-armed bandit. They laughed so as to be heard above the noise of a crowd of people crushed suddenly into a small space, even above the steam-organ hurdy-gurdy noises. The hobby-horses, all mounted, circled, the redhead sidesaddle. The rising-and-falling mountain range beyond the bay was hidden by a pitch-black cloud that came down like a smothering curtain. Then the curtain was split by forked lightning and the thunder came before the flash had faded. Under the wooden roof of the place of hobby-horses and bandits it was then so dark that one of the showmen switched on the lights. More lightning, the thunder seemed to come closer. A woman screamed and more children than you could count or kill began to cry. The elder of the two laughing sisters turned round and looked at us, and began to laugh as if she had just learned the secret. No question or doubt about it, nor was there any point in mentioning the matter to Eunan—but she was laughing at us.

Dolores is a slender sensitive woman who paints well and exhibits and sells her paintings. Gene, in spite of an English surname, has Arab blood in him that makes him look like a non-aggressive, even affable, slightly smaller version of General Nasser. On Saturday afternoons Rich's in Lennox Square in Atlanta, Georgia, is as good a field as I've ever seen for the wholehearted bird-watcher. Gene and Dolores couldn't see him, but Eunan of the Glen, lost to me long ago by the Donegal sea, was beside me on the escalator on the way up to the shoe department. He was so real to me that day, for the first time in 27 years, that I was ready to speak to him out loud, ready to hear him say: No, Bernard, not that one. She couldn't be a modest girl. Look at the bare back of her. Be the holy, if the parish priest saw the like of that on a teacher's wife in the Glen of Glenties, there'd be a new teacher in the school before the end of the month if not sooner.

Yet Eunan—it must have been something he read—had desired, I think, silks and perfumes with the sins he imagined and feared: and the silks and perfumes were all here. It was the women of his own mountainy place and people that he feared most. He told me of a girl who grabbed his hand in the darkness of the schoolhouse at a travelling movie show: She had a palm, Bernard, as hard as a whinstone rock. It would frighten you. A woman shouldn't be like that. A woman should be gentle. And true. Terrible things, Bernard, can happen to country schoolmasters. A man I heard tell of got into trouble with the girls in the school, two of them, and one was jealous of the other, and she told. The country girls are deceitful. And if you married the wrong one your job's ruined.

Looking up the escalator at the bare-backed beauty ahead of us, I said that you could play the zither on the knuckles of her spine.

She was a tall olive Amazonian, with her right shoulder arrogantly bare, and white pants so tight that her bottom looked like an outsize meringue; and a crimson waistcoat all front and no back, that was a miracle of cantilever.

But it was Gene, not Eunan, that heard. Bundoran was 27 years away, and 4,000 miles.

—Hardly worth while, he said, for her escort to take her home. Nothing more left to see. Billy Graham says that it's okay for girls to wear miniskirts if there is no intention of provoking sensual desire.

Oh Eunan McAtavey where are you now?

Failure after failure, he wouldn't take the jump, so there was nothing for it now but the Palais de Danse. As a man I know says: If you want to get it you must go where it is.

Miss Kerrigan would say to me: You're more cheerful now, Bernard, since Eunan came. You're not thinking long any more. I'm so glad the two of you get along together. Good healthy walks, bracing breezes, silvery sands.

Everybody in the bloody place seemed to know that jingle off by heart.

—Booming breakers, lovely lands, rhymed my mother.

—That's real poetry, she said smugly and just to madden me for she knew that I kept hidden in my room above the harbour the steadily accumulating collected works: three developing epics, one on Barac, Deborah and King Sisera in the *Book of Judges*, one on the Easter Rising of 1916, one on the lighting by St Patrick, on the Hill of Slane, of Ireland's first-ever Pascal fire. Apart of course, from many shorter pieces of an intense lyricism, inspired by one or other or all of the chosen nine: Could I into that silent shrine advance, to where the sacred flame makes all things plain, what joy were mine to find engraven there my name.

—Good healthy walks, said Miss Kerrigan. But don't overdo it. Think of your back and all that lying down and standing up for ordination.

She was right: I mean about the thinking long. For I had now an interest in life outside myself, and was more anxious that Eunan should find his woman, and find engraven there his name, than he was himself. He had nothing: my hoard or pocket of nine nurses was in Dublin beyond the mountains, I could afford to be generous. For to be afflicted by desire for hoaching Scottish lasses, and yet not be able to say a blessed preliminary word to any one of them must have been pain beyond pain. Once in a while he would whisper, spluttering sideways into my ear, gripping my bicep hard enough to hurt, as if he were trying to hold himself back from leaping on the lady there and then: That one, Bernard. That's the ticket. God, it would be something to give her a run for it in the sandhills.

Nearly always the desired one was pale, golden-haired, prim, modestly dressed and an obvious member of the Children of Mary. This puzzled me for a while until I realized sadly that Eunan, perhaps subconsciously, was attracted to young women whose appearance would please the parish priest. When I managed to put chat on one of these votaresses Eunan was no help at all: arms dangling, mouth like a vice, gaze at a tangent—towards the breakers, or the bulk of Truskmore concealing Ben Bulben, or the cliffs of Slieve League across the bay. So there was nothing for it but the Palais de Danse where not even a shy buck like Eunan would have a chance of escape, for far and wide the place was notorious for frenzied women. Even the boom-thump-boom-thump-boom of it, echoing night after night from the sea to the hills and back again was the cause of protests and letters to the local paper.

—See it, Eunan, you must. If you went back to Glenties and said you'd never seen the inside of the palais they'd laugh at you. They'd do worse. They'd worry about you.

The palais had also the name for being a rough class of a place. There was a long-nosed man I knew from my own town, who kept the entire works of Edgar Wallace in a tin trunk under his bed, and had got mildly drunk one night in the palais and had bones broken by the gorillas. Not a word of this did I tell to Eunan, he was nervous enough as it was, nor was I all that happy myself: shiny tight black suit and creaking back-splint smelling like horse-harness weren't exactly standard equipment for the palais. What would I say to the first girl who put her arm around me to convince her that I wasn't made of leather or wood, or about to perish with a petrifying disease?

We crossed the strand. A mist-swollen moon was coming up

slowly from behind Truskmore. The surf shone, the cliff-shadows were jet-black on the sand, the small stream that dribbled across the strand was silver. The glaring lights, the boom-thump-boom of the palais were sacrilege. Restive Eunan at any moment might turn and bolt like a colt running from harness and, if he did, I'd have no power to halt him. For now that I was face-to-face with the palais I was damned near as nervous as he was, and not much more of a man of the world. Nearer and nearer. The entering crowd shuffled around a doorway guarded by the two gorillas who had beaten up the long-nosed devotee of Edgar Wallace. The lights were blinding, the noise deafening. Eunan was moving more slowly, had, indeed, almost come to a halt, when a woman's voice said clearly into my ear: Is it going to say Mass you are, your reverence? Or has somebody had a sudden heart-attack?

It was the laughing girl. She was still laughing. So was her sister. They were linked, and leaning against each other with unaffected gaiety.

—It's no place for a clerical student, the elder sister said.

—An ex-clerical student.

—A clerical error, then.

They laughed fit to fall at the ancient joke and I couldn't but laugh with them, while Eunan stood there as stiff as my back-splint.

—There was a fight in there already, she said.

The younger sister, as I recall, never spoke, but only laughed.

—Drunken animals. The civic guards took away two that you couldn't see for blood.

She took my arm: Let's go for a walk to Tullaghan. There's a lovely moon.

Tullaghan was two miles to the side of the town away from the Fairy Bridges and my four-cornered wooden shelter. A concrete pathway led along the tops of low cliffs, the sea to the right, quiet residential hotels to the left. Beyond the rock bathing-pool that was reserved for nuns the hotels ended and there was nothing but grass, grey-white under the moon, and the moon shining on the water.

—I'm Ellen, she said. That there behind is Madge, my sister. We'd be twins only she's two years younger.

Behind us in the salty moonlight Madge was laughing gently but continuously, Eunan wasn't making even a grunt, and it was a wonder to God to me that he had come walking at all: except to escape from the more certain horrors of the palais.

—She's very like you. Except that she laughs more.

—We both laugh a lot. But Madge laughs more because she's shy.

—She's in proper company this blessed night.

—He does look shy, too. Where's he from?

—The hills of Donegal.

—All night and day I'm dreaming, she sang, of the hills of Donegal.

Then she said: We're from the meadows of Fermanagh, from Lisbellaw.

Lisbellaw I knew, as I knew even then the half of Ireland: Lisbellaw, and the sleepy lake shore and grass meadows all around. The map shows a filigree pattern of blue, Upper Lough Erne, on a field of flat green: restful country, quiet towns, little harbours with long names where you could idle away ten life-times fishing spoon or spinning minnow for pike and perch and bream. It made me warm to her right away that she came from a countryside meant for laziness or, since I was literary then, lotus-eating. She swung easily on my arm, and sometimes went one, two, three and a one, two, three on the tips of her toes as if she were readying to dance the Walls of Limerick. So I slipped my arm around her waist and felt like the hell of an ex-cleric, and hoped I was giving good example to Eunan lumbering along behind us.

She was wearing a green sort of dress, not a raincoat as when she had first surfaced in the place of the one-armed bandits. She had a small golden-coloured harp as a clasp at the cleavage, no beret, her dark hair dry and shampoo-shiny, and held in place by a golden-coloured snood; nor did she smell of peat smoke as it was generally said that rural beauties did. Thus, we came to the old square tower that guards the eel-weir at Bundrowes, where the Drowes, which is a magic river, meets the sea, and all the wonder of Tullaghan Strand was before us: no ordinary level of sand where people went bathing, but rank upon rank of oval stones that the sea had shaped. They shone, between salt and moonshine, like gigantic jewels. All along the country roads out of Bundoran, into Donegal and Leitrim and Sligo, you could see Tullaghan stones painted all colours and making borders for beds in flower gardens.

Ellen and myself sat in the shadow of the tower and looked out on the flashing Drowes where the trout have the gizzards of chickens because of a miracle performed by a saint back there at Lough Melvin where the river comes from. She said that when she and Madge went back to Lisbellaw they'd take Tullaghan stones with them, and paint them striped, and keep them as souvenirs of this lovely night. That set us kissing and grappling merrily in the shadows. When we came up for air she asked: Where are they?

Oh, there they were, sure enough, not rolling on the grass or wrestling in the shadows but standing 50 yards from us on the bank of the Drowes, and five yards from each other: Eunan, a dark statue, arms by its side, that looked as if it had been there as long as the tower. They were too far away for us to hear if Madge were still laughing. Since there was nothing, short of roping them together, that we could do about it, we kissed and grappled again and when we had surfaced again they were exactly as we had last seen them, enchanted to stone by magic river and sea and moon. Ellen breathed a long breath and slowly let it loose again. She said: They'd never credit it in Lisbellaw.

—Ellen, I know a song about Lisbellaw.

—Sing it, for God's sake.

—It's in Irish.

—Sing it in Irish.

So I sang in Irish the verse that mentions Lisbellaw.

—What does it mean?

—Something like this: I met a fairy woman down at Lisbellaw and asked her would any key unlock the lock of love. In low and kind and gentle voice she answered me: When love locks the heart the lock will never be loosened.

—It would be grand, she said, but I doubt if it's true.

We kissed again, quietly and without grappling. She stood up and smoothed down the green dress and said we'd better walk home before Madge froze to death or leaped in the Drowes for lack of anything better to do.

The fighting was over for the night in the Palais de Danse. The long moonlit town, painted all colours for the holiday season, was asleep, it seemed, and silent, except that you could guess that here and there and everywhere it was still a holiday and the fun was going on. We left the sisters at the door of their boarding-house. Because of Eunan, or rather because of Madge, I forbore kissing Ellen good-night, but she understood, and gripped my hand hard, and dug her nails into my palm, and said we'd meet tomorrow night by the hobby-horses, and hoped that the moon would be out again.

Eunan and myself walked wordless home along the bright empty street. It wasn't until we were at Miss Kerrigan's door that he spoke: Bernard, she had a very hard hand.

I said nothing.

—That one, Bernard, was laughing at me all night.

—Not at you, Eunan. She was laughing because she's young and on her holidays.

After a while I added: And walking out with a young man by the bright silvery light of the moon.

—Bernard, ever since the first day I went to school country girls have been laughing at me.

Up in my silent room I couldn't even read myself to sleep, feeling sorrier then for lonely Eunan than out at Tullaghan I had felt for laughing Madge.

The morn was breaking fresh and fair and the lark sang in the sky, and it was as lovely a day as you would expect after such a night of moonlight. Eunan and myself walked like automatons across the strand. What, I asked myself, are the wild waves saying, for Eunan hadn't a word to throw to land or ocean, nor could I think of anything to say that wouldn't make the poor man more miserable than he obviously was already. In sad silence we came to the two high flights of wooden steps that went up from a moist cliff-shadowed corner of the strand to the top of Roguey. Eunan climbed up ahead of me—as blithely as a man climbing to the scaffold. He had his pinstripe on and his trousers, God help me, seemed to have shrunk. Up above us there was music and dancing and singing voices. The local branch of the Gaelic League kept an open-air dancing-floor at that point on the clifftop, and all day long, Maryanne, weather permitting, the young people were at it hammer and tongs: slip jig and hornpipe and fourteen-hand reel, the Walls of Limerick, the Waves of Tory, Saddle the Pony, the Mason's Apron and the Chaffpool Post. It was such a lively place and such a beautiful morning. Far out, wisps of mist drifted over dark-blue unbroken water. There was autumn in the air. The flat-topped mountains were still hidden. Because of the noise of the music and dancing the cries from the strand were inaudible, so that the silent movements of the people on the edge of the surf, and of the donkeys and the baby elephant, seemed completely senseless. White mist, too, drifted in bundles over the golf-links, and the clockwork figures stepping out of the mist, vanishing into it again were crazily comic.

It was part of the mood of the morning that I should at that moment see the blonde and purple woman, 50 yards away, higher up the slope on the path to the Fairy Bridges. She sat quite close to the cliff's edge. She waved and I waved in return.

—Who is that? says Eunan.

—What we're after, Eunan. Scottish and glamorous. Look at that purple dress, that blonde hair.

The blonde hair shone in the morning. She waved again.

—That there's no laughing country girl, Eunan. Perfume, I'd say, that would flatten a regiment. If there was a wind this morning we'd get the perfume already.

Side-by-side, keeping step, we advanced up the slope. Behind us the dancing and music went on as if we never had been. His big feet beside me were no longer flopping in brothel creepers but solid and determined in square-toed black shoes. The woman was reading a

book, her head turned away from us. At 60 paces it was clear that I
had been right about the perfume.

—Good-morning, I said.

It was an irreproachable and perfectly accurate remark.

She turned her head and looked at us and said: To whom have I
the honour of speaking?

It wasn't that she was old: remembering her now I suppose she
couldn't have been more than 60. She wore red shoes and purple
stockings, and her short purple dress, tucked up to allow her to
squat in comfort, showed fat knees with pads of surplus flesh to the
insides of the kneecaps. It wasn't that she was ugly. It was the
desperate effort to defeat ugliness that made me feel that life could
be a losing battle. She wore a loose purple jacket about as long as
the dress, and a striped blouse—I can't remember the colour of the
stripes—and a foamy sort of syllabubbly chiffon scarf emerging
from the neckline of the dress, which was cut like a schoolgirl's
gym-frock. That now was what she wore, for she was the sort of
woman that you looked first at the radiant clothes before you came
face to face with her face. On her left hand she seemed to wear two
wedding rings and an engagement ring and a keeper. She had fine
plump hands. But the face was a mask, with long false lashes and,
below the eyes, radiating black streaks that looked as if they had
been done with a sharp knife dipped in cobbler's dye. The eyes,
which were not unkind, moved almost audibly when they moved at
all. It wasn't that we were disappointed in her, it was my awful
feeling that she too had her dreams and that the pair of us did not
fulfil them.

Her voice, I will confess, was a little shrill and she had, in so far
as I could judge, a Lancashire way of speaking which is fine in its
own way but you want to know English very well to keep up with it.
To this day I can see her quite clearly, apart from the colours of the
stripes in her blouse, and I remember her with interest and a great
curiosity. I can even hear her talking—about her husband who was
coming to Bundoran to join her. She was a fit rival for the mysteri-
ous Atlantic which was at that moment her background: oceans of
woman, all waiting for daring young mariners.

But Eunan, like Bishop Berkeley, thought otherwise. He was already ten yards away and moving fast while I was preparing to squat beside her, even though squatting in a back-splint was a trick that took some rehearsing.

—My husband, she said, had a special sort of tandem bicycle built all to his own specifications. We frequently take trips on it.

At least that's what I thought she said. But what between the Lancashire accent and the state of confusion in which Eunan's retreat left me, I could have imagined the words: they didn't seem very likely. There he went, his arms stiff as logs, his trouser-bottoms halfways to his knees.

—What's wrong with your friend? she said. Was he short-taken?

She laughed fit to frighten the gulls and, since I couldn't think of anything to say and couldn't laugh with her, I fled. Her laughter followed me. My back-splint seemed to have slipped its moorings, but that also was imagination. Truskmore was pushing one jagged rocky shoulder out of the mist. Come and cover me, oh mist, hide me from that laughter, and hell run away with Eunan McAtavey who could at least have stood his ground until, with dignity, we retreated together. But when I came on him in the crowd by the dancing-floor he looked so hapless that I could find no word of reproach.

—An error of judgement, Eunan, I said, She looked all right from a distance.

—They all do.

The dancers were having the time of their lives. Nobody paid the least attention to us.

—That's the sort of woman, he said, that you're warned against in the catechism.

—You're from a different diocese, Eunan. The catechism where I came from never mentioned the likes of her.

—She was mentioned somewhere if it wasn't in the catechism.

We walked on by the freshwater spring and the Fairy Bridges and the four-cornered shelter in which, to my annoyance, there was a young couple holding hands and gazing out to sea: Head out to sea when on your lee the breakers you discern. Oh, adieu to all the billowy coasts.

We crossed Tullan Strand with its gulls and curlews, and crossed the sand-dunes and walked the long street to Lios na Mara and didn't swap a word all the way. Up in my room I opened my neglected books, took notebook and pencil and set to the reading: this was my business, I was a frost and a failure as a man of the world and, as a pimp, quite preposterous. He was so silent at lunch and again at high tea, ham salad, that I knew Miss Kerrigan and my mother thought we had had a row, but were too polite to say anything about it; and that night there was no moon and no Eunan.

The morning mist had dissolved into mizzling rain. He hadn't even told Miss Kerrigan that he was going. Without any feeling in her voice my mother said: I hope you weren't rude to him. He was so shy.

The lights around the hurdy-gurdies were bleary weeping eyes. The hobby-horses, riderless, went round a few times, then halted hopelessly, and their music stopped and there was no sound between the sea and the mountains but the boom-thump-boom of the palais. I wore a heavy black cloth coat and a black hat and looked, Ellen said, like a parish priest on the run. With a rain-coated girl on each arm I walked as far as the four-cornered shelter. The weather was telling us that the holidays were over and that everything came to an end.

—He ran away from us, Ellen said. He was afraid of the fairy women of Lisbellaw.

When I told them about the purple blonde on the clifftop they laughed for ten minutes, and went on laughing at the idea of Eunan, suitcase in hand, legging it back to the mountainy safety of the Vale of Dibbin. In the four-cornered shelter I profited by his absence and made gentle love to the two of them. Oh, it was all very harmless: running from one corner to another, grappling, kissing, with two girls who couldn't stop laughing; discovering that shy Madge was far and away the more ardent of the two. We walked back through rising wind that blew the clamour of the palais off towards Lough Melvin. The town was a long line of weeping lights. When we came as far as the hobby-horses, the music—although the animals were at rest—was playing about the old rustic bridge by the mill, and Ellen and Madge sang:

> But one day we parted in pain and regret,
> Our vows then we could not fulfill.

—Too true, Ellen said, We're off tomorrow.

—But you'll write, Madge said.

—And we'll meet again next year, Ellen said.

—Maybe, said Madge, you might come to see us in Lisbellaw.

Although I meant to write, I never did: Dublin and the nine, and other things, distracted me. The next year I wasn't in Bundoran; and although ten years later I passed briefly through Lisbellaw, there was another woman with me and I never even thought of Madge and Ellen. As I said, if it hadn't been for the ancient blonde on the green in Atlanta I'd never even have remembered Eunan.

A beautiful blonde girl sat in a chair and in the most queenly fashion allowed herself to be fitted with pink shoes. A serious youth, he couldn't have been more than eighteen, knelt at her feet and did the fitting. She was searching for a shoe of a colour that would match some detail in the dress she wore. Patiently the young fellow eased the dainty foot into shoe after shoe after shoe. We marvelled at his restraint.

—What, Gene said, is behind the American rape epidemic?

That had been a joke between us, not a very good one, ever since we had seen the question printed on the cover of a lurid magazine, and with it the picture of a man with billiard-ball eyes roping a buxom, and quite unconcerned, lady to a chair. We were still guessing at answers, and watching the young kneeling troubadour and the girl of the pink shoes, when Dolores returned. We drove back to my place. The aged blonde was gone from the green.

On that very day my mother was writing me a letter. That sort of coincidence is common. For instance, on a day in a college in Virginia when a student was asking me about a friend of mine, a singer, he, in Chicago, was mailing me his newest long-player.

My mother wrote:

Miss Kerrigan, whom you may recall, died recently and I went to Bundoran to the funeral. May she rest in peace. She was a dear woman, albeit a little eccentric, and thought the world and all of you, and thought in her final doting days that you were a priest and wondered why you never came to see her. I always told her you were far away on the foreign missions and that the Jesuits were very strict and didn't allow you home often. It wasn't much of a lie, and I feel that God and even the Jesuits would forgive me. She prayed for you every night. But who should be at the funeral only your companion of long ago, Eunan McAtavey, with his wife and nine children, a car-load of them. They seemed very happy. He was asking for you. He said he read everything you wrote, in newspapers and even in books.

On what dusty lovely Donegal roadway, walking home from school or Mass or market-day shopping, did he, or how did he, manage to tell a girl that he loved her?

They seemed very happy, she said. He was asking for me. He had read everything I had written. Ah well, his memory was better than mine. He couldn't very well explain to my mother and his wife why he ran, or what he ran, or thought he was running, from. What ever became, I wonder, of the fairy women of Lisbellaw?

ELM VALLEY VALERIE

ONE SATURDAY morning my Aunt Brigid said to me that she doubted if Valerie would ever marry that horrid Mr Craig from London. Twelve months previously my Uncle Owen, who lived up in the mountains and lilted, said that if Brigid came home from Philadelphia he would raise the roof. She had been 50 years almost in the United States. Owen meant that to celebrate her return he would add another storey to his long white farmhouse, a meeting-place for musicians in that part of the country. His own lilting or mouth music was part of the entertainment that went on there and it was told that, when he was a young fellow and going to the country dances, he had, because the fiddler fell ill, lilted all night at a dance to keep the dancers going.

My mother, who sang ballads, was very proud of that achievement of her brother's youth and told the story any time she had a chance. He was a tall man with a red moustache and a long bouncing stride. With a sharp knife and any old broken branch he could carve you nearly anything you'd mention from a primitive statue to a whistle that would play tunes. He did raise the roof, too, or he got two fiddlers and a melodeon player and a journeyman carpenter who played the flute and a plasterer who was a piper to help him to do it. Music, we are told, built the towers of Troy. Aunt Brigid did come home from Philadelphia. She was 68.

She taught a lot of us to play euchre which was her favourite card-game, as with Bret Harte's Heathen Chinee which I wish to remark and my language is plain. Her favourite delicacy was a sort of a grey soup frozen to semi-solidity and archipelagoed with slivers of dead and butchered chickens. When she had her own house in our town for a while every visitor calling to see her had to take a spoonful or two of the stuff which was supposed to do something for you. It made most people queasy. As for myself I grew to like it because I liked her and I'd do anything for a friend.

For her first three months in Ireland she lived with us. That's how I know that like the best generals on long-ago battlefields she owned a portable toilet which she delicately called a commode, an object of polished wood that I thought was a cabinet gramophone until, sneaking around one day when the house was empty, I opened it. When the news got around the neighbourhood, as it did, though not through me, its existence caused some comment, and neighbours visiting the house were always anxious, though they were too polite to say so, to sneak up and have a peep: when the owner was out, that is, and the object not in use. In our world in Ulster in those days nobody locked doors, or needed to.

—Valerie's aunt, she said to me, doesn't approve of the cinema.

My eyes were on *Allen's Latin Grammar, ante apud ad adversus circum circa citra cis.* My mind was in the murderous swamp with the *Master of Ballantrae* about whom I had been reading the night before until the fire crumbled and, with the rest of the house abed and with the creeps the story had given me, I'd been afraid to go out in the dark, to fill the scuttle. My heart was in the highlands ten miles from the town, chasing the wild deer and following the roe, and chatting up the American female cousin of a schoolfriend of mine who lived up there and cycled every day to school, twelve miles there and, of course, twelve miles back. The female cousin and her gold-toothed father were vacationing. It was the season for romance.

It was a sunny Saturday morning and three hours school were ahead of me, like a smoky hazardous tunnel. Aunt Brigid's voice came to me as it always did on Saturday mornings from the heart of some numinous cloud. But I had developed a knack of hearing and answering without really listening: what she said I more or less heard but it was always of something else I was thinking. She talked at speed and didn't much bother about responses. I said: That's a bit old-fashioned, isn't it, even for them?

—They're old-fashioned people. Of Huguenot origin, the father's people, weavers and Protestants who came to Ireland from France more than 200 years ago. Her mother was real French and

very beautiful it was said. She met Valerie's father when she was a
nurse at the western front and he was a young officer in the Irish
Guards. They say that she had that grace and charm transmitted
down the decades by women of her family softening the rather
narrow-minded outlook which Valerie's father inherited from
Puritan forebears.

Decades of the holy rosary I had heard about and, when the
family knelt together for prayers, participated in. Decades of
women was an idea that needed some grappling with. But what the
hell and *ante apud ad adversus*. The colonel, Aunt Brigid, doesn't look
to me as if anything ever had softened him.

Like a statue set in motion the retired colonel went through the
town on his high green bicycle, three-speed gear on the cross-bar,
salmon gear on his back. His knees went up and down like parts of
machinery. He looked neither to right nor left. He seldom spoke.
He nodded to the occasional person but made no distinctions in
religion or social rank: he nodded just when he happened to notice
somebody was there and he seldom noticed anybody. He looked
much too old to be his daughter's father. She must then have been
in her middle twenties and looked like all the world was lovely to
men approaching or a little past the crisis of eighteen.

—She was reared in a château, Valerie's mother that is.

Château, *circum, circa, citra, cis*, didn't convey a lot to me, yet it
was accepted that people who were reared in châteaux couldn't
look or feel too easily at home in either of the town's two cinemas.
One of them was a corrugated iron shed, painted red and called the
Galaxy Kinema. To get into the other one you had to pass through
the backyard of an hotel, the backyard being, in that transitional
period of the world's history, half stableyard and half garage: so
that above the music of the songs of the time, like Tiptoe through
the Tulips and Sonny Boy, you heard the stamping of hooves and
the thunderous backfiring of primitive engines. In the Galaxy
Kinema the projector broke down every twenty minutes or so with
such interesting regularity that a blank white screen was accepted
as part of the programme and no longer even inspired obscenities
in the wits who sat on hard wooden benches in what was aptly

called the Pit. Once though, the machine clogged and the screen didn't go blank. Harry Carey, as the man with the badge, was left, gun in each hand, in the act of leaping from a two-storey hotel to crash, guns blazing, through the roof of a one-storey bank and so to interrupt a robbery. There he was like Mahomet's tomb for a good ten minutes or so before gravity resumed her reign, and some of the advice proffered to him from the Pit I can still remember.

In the picture-palace above the stable-garage breakdowns were less to be relied on and when they did happen a fat fiddler in a leather motoring-coat played music to while away the time. In the days of the silent film that same fat fiddler stood behind the screen and made noises that were called effects: like rattling thin sheets of tin to simulate the guns at the battle of Mons.

No!—châteaux on the splendid Loire or anywhere else had nothing to do with all that, and I had never seen Valerie in either of those places. But I saw her that Saturday morning, on my way to school and she smiled as she passed me by. She smiled much as her father nodded, as if vaguely aware that the world was out there somewhere. Except that, unlike her father, she was beautiful, a rather large woman, blonde hair down her back, eyes like lakes where regiments of guardsmen could drown, complexion all peaches and roses and cream, as God is my judge no other way to describe it. Like her father she went on a bicycle. Her bicycle always seemed to be too low for her and the thought of her thighs moving up and down under her navy pleated skirt used to send us all into frenzies of lust. A wickerwork basket on the handlebars overflowed with magazines. A wickerwork basket at the back of the saddle was all groceries and things. She smiled at all, perhaps she smiled all the time. A chemist in our town who had once won a prize for looking like Rudolf Valentino said she was the most beautiful woman in the world. An Irish setter trotted behind her, tongue out like the rest of us. The chemist said: She walks in beauty like the night.

Surely to Christ a man who looked like Rudolf Valentino should know what he was talking about. But not like the night, like the sun dancing on Easter Sunday morning. God, those secret thighs, that pleated skirt, those adorable flat-heeled yellow brogues. Up and down, up and down, oh to be a saddle of her bike. That morning, still shaken, I said to my pal Alec: Valerie smiled at me.

He said: Don't worry. There are funnier-looking men in the town than you.

That annoyed me so much that I never told him a word of all that Aunt Brigid had told me: among other things, that Valerie's mother had been a reputed beauty in the most aristocratic circles in Paris and that, like many French women, she made her own clothes. That pleated skirt. That sky-blue jacket. Oh to be her Irish setter scenting forever her fragrance down the wind: a big girl but beautiful.

We are by no means a mercenary people. Aunt Brigid, a small dainty woman with glass beads on the ruched bosom of her dark modest dress, had a lot of dollars with her when she came home from the States. She was, as I said, 68. We hoped she would be with us for years, moving restlessly as she did from one relative's house to that of another, lodging with people who were no relations, retiring for a while into a home for old ladies—they were all too old or ill or tiresome for her—finally setting up house on her own in the village of Drumgoole, about ten miles from the town. She had been for so long among strangers in a faraway land that she found it difficult to settle. We understood this and wished her joy and, I repeat, hoped that she would be with us for years to come. Yet if the Almighty in his infinite goodness deigned to call her to himself, saying well done thou good and faithful servant, well then the dollars were always there and wouldn't go to waste.

The Almighty deigned to do nothing of the sort. She lived to see 90 plus and to dispose elegantly of 99 per cent of her own dollars. One frosty Christmas morning when she was over 80 she broke both legs on the ice when walking to Mass. The bones knit again as if she had been eighteen. To her last hour she could sip and enjoy a glass of whiskey as large as herself for (as happens) she became smaller with age: and devil the effect the whiskey ever had on her except to give her eyes a sparkle and to set spots of girlish blushes

on her cheeks. She was a great lovable lady and with great last in
her and one Saturday morning she said rather sharply: Oh Mr
Craig I hate you. Of course I can see that you have your disap-
pointments and scruples. You're deeply in love with a young
woman who has grown very dear to you. You see perfectly well that
she doesn't care for you. She likes you just the way she should like a
distant cousin, which you are.

—But marriage is a different matter. Then there's the house and
the land, so much more spacious than what you're used to in
London.

There was nobody to be seen in the room except Aunt Brigid and
myself. Out in the scullery my mother was singing and rattling,
taps flowing. Perhaps Craig was, like James Durie the Master of
Ballantrae, here when he was there, dead and alive at the same
time. If he had suddenly materialized, then slowly faded until
nothing was left but his smile or scowl or look of perplexity or
agonized love, then at least I'd have known what he looked like. By
sight I knew the colonel's nod and Valerie's smile: but nothing at
all about Craig, although his living most of the time in London,
and the rest of the time in the large, remote, park-surrounded
house that, shell for the pearl, contained the perfections, clothed
and, ah God, unclothed, of Valerie, would rationally account for
that.

At the far end of the town from the place where we lived you
came to the crossroads called the Gusset. Why the Gusset, God
knew: the place had nothing to do with tailoring or dressmaking,
and I remember it only for two things. Once there by the light of a
street lamp I saw a tiny bewildered lizard, the sort we called
man-eaters and that were found only in bogs and marshes. By
precocious zoologists it was commonly held that if one of them
caught you with your mouth open it would jump down your throat
and refuse to come out again. But that little lizard was lost, had
crawled up a drain and through a grating or something and was
clearly wondering how he had got there, how he was going to get
back to where he came from. Three or four ragamuffins, mouths

defensively closed, were on hands and knees poking him with twigs. Their silence added to the oddity of the scene.

Alec and myself rescued him, dropped him down the grating and hoped for the best. We never saw him again, and a lizard lost by lamplight has stayed in my memory as a symbol of loneliness and bewilderment.

The other thing about the Gusset was that one of the four roads that went out from the cross was a private road and led to the house that Valerie lived in. Groups of young aspiring men used to gather at the Gusset to see her cycling past. Or parade in the evenings as far up the private road as was possible which was what Alec and myself had been up to the night we rescued the lizard.

That road, surfaced with a rare sort of red gravel, served three big houses in all, Valerie's house being the biggest and the most remote from the ordinary ways of men. The gravel added an extra touch of fairyland enchantment. At least three stern notices reminded you that the place was private. The house stood on a slope, dark trees behind it, lawns in front sloping down to a bend of the river. Across the water bugles sounded from behind the grey walls of the barracks. It was a fitting place for an enchantress to live in and, naturally and alas, we knew it only from a distance. Like Valerie's smile and her father's nod it was remote. Anything could be going on in that fastness: Craig's despicable, semi-senile infatuation, the tyranny of a martinet of an aunt. In a way we knew so little about her beyond her smile: and the young women who went to the Loreto convent or the Protestant academy couldn't have helped us with information even if we had humiliated ourselves to the point of asking them. She hadn't ever been to convent or academy but to a finishing school in France and to another finishing school in the Isle of Wight. Twice finished, we thought, and oh God, who had had the pleasure. We were vague about what went on in finishing schools.

Bugles sounded across the river. Troops marched to Aldershot and India, and returned. Pipes played the Inniskilling Dragoon and Adieu to Belashanny. It was to be expected that Valerie might fall in love with an officer. Yet it was not a good Saturday morning,

with autumn coming on and heavy rains, when Aunt Brigid said:
The young officer has gone to see Miss Meredith, the aunt you
know.

I hadn't known but I knew now as the Lord God, more or less,
said, according to the kirk preacher, to the sinners pleading previous ignorance from the pit of hellfire. Very poorly I felt as I
listened. Felt even sorry for Craig as against the unnamed officer.
Craig was old and stiff and far down the field, but what hell chance
had any of us against a man who, pipes playing, could lead men all
the way to India.

—Miss Meredith, of course, is an awful snob. She hardly speaks
to Lady Cromlin because although Lady Cromlin married a lord
she was a vulgar person to begin with. The captain . . .

So he was a full captain.

— . . . will need to have his credentials in order. He regards
Valerie as a being from another and higher planet suddenly
descended upon this weary and desolate world.

So did we all: he was no better than the rest of us.

—Miss Meredith is very stern. Her only true love was killed in
the hunting field. She was never in a bus.

The rains passed and were followed by mellow light. One Saturday
morning I read out loud: The trees are in their autumn beauty, the
woodland paths are dry.

And read the poem all the way to the end: By what lake's edge or
pool delight men's eyes when I awake some day to find they have
flown away?

She listened to me with more attention than I had ever given to
her and I had the decency to feel a little ashamed. With the tiniest
of white lace handkerchiefs and the tip of the forefinger of her right
hand she picked little drops of moisture from the corners of her
eyes. For the first time I noticed that her face, though unwrinkled
and bright as a pippin, was very small. On the wall above her
where she sat in the corner between the table, at which she had just
finished her breakfast, and my four shelves of books, there was a
favourite picture of mine: seven highland cattle by a mountain

river and, in the background, a great blue shoulder of mountain. My heart's in the highlands, my heart is not here.

—That's a beautiful poem, she said, and you read it very well. It would be lovely to see the lake where the swans were. You see I saw so much of America and so little of Ireland. I never even saw Dublin.

She sipped at another cup of tea. My mother had gone out to somebody's funeral and from the high steeple the dead bell was tolling over the town. The book of poems I closed and went on reading to myself what J. B. Priestley had written about *Angel Pavement*. Her voice was high up and faraway as if she had taken wings and flown, a tiny black bird glistening with beads, to the top of that blue mountain.

—Dr Haughton, she said or seemed to me to say, has always congratulated Valerie on the roses in her cheeks. But the roses, I fear, may soon be faded. Miss Meredith didn't take to the captain and he thought Miss Meredith was like something out of Charles Dickens or Mrs Henry Wood.

Dickens I knew all about and as for Mrs Henry Wood, well a travelling company had once brought East Lynne all the way to the drinking and gambling den known as the Hall of the Irish National Foresters, a friendly and benevolent society. Not one of them would ever have been sober enough to recognize a forest if it came at him like Birnam Wood. Dead, dead and never called me mother. That was East Lynne for you.

—Valerie's trouble for a whole week has been to get away from Craig so as to be able to see the captain in secret. One thundery evening she even went to bed with her nightdress on over her clothes, and later slipped out to meet him and got caught in a downpour and drenched.

—All the ladies, Aunt Bee assured me, love a uniform because it makes a man look more like a man.

In so far as J. B. Priestley would allow me, I thought: The hell with Valerie and the gallant captain, their world is not for me, not for us, not for decrepit Craig whoever or wherever he is.

That morning, anyway, my heart was not so much in the highlands as far out on the heaving billow. Vacationing was ended and the grey-eyed, sylph-like cousin of my mountainy schoolfriend had taken ship with her father at Cobh and by that moment must be far beyond the reach of those south-western Irish headlands that stretch out to welcome or to say farewell. In those days of reverie it wasn't all that easy to know exactly who or what one was in love with.

—But love at first sight, said Aunt Brigid, is lightning as the French say. The captain squared up his shoulders in a gesture well known to his fellow-officers and faced up to Miss Meredith. But to no avail. Unalterable hostility. And the minister's daughter has always encouraged her to strike out and make a career for herself. And the inevitable has happened.

At that dramatic moment my eyes and some portion of my mind turned from *Angel Pavement* to Aunt Bee and the wild river, the highland cattle, the blue mountain.

—Valerie, she said, has turned her back on the lot of them and flown to Belgium to distant relatives of her mother.

Well that was that, and it wasn't likely or possible that Alec or myself or the throng who waited with little hope at the crossroads of the Gusset would follow her to brave the opposition of every smiling, scented, bowing-and-scraping man among the Belgians. She was further away than the girl tossing on the Atlantic billow. It never occurred to me that in Belgium or anywhere else there could be a woman the equal of Valerie, that Belgian men might have eyes for other visions. We had lost her forever: the way you see a beautiful girl in a city bus, and you look at her and she looks at you and your eyes meet for a moment, and you know you will never see her again. *Allen's Latin Grammar* told me that pity, remember and forget govern the genitive set. The last word I suppose, was stuck in to make an easily memorizable rhyme. Allen worked that way.

All very wise for my age, except that as, on that blessed morning, I walked to school for a new and my last term she rode her bicycle right under my bows when I was crossing John Street and nerving my thighs and lungs for the steep ascent, under high spires, of

Church Hill. She was as large as life, as large and beautiful as herself. No less than three red setters, one of them little more than a pup, tongues out, enjoying the morning as dogs do, trotted behind her. The basket before her overflowed with magazines. The basket behind her was a bright mound of oranges and grapefruit held in place by a sort of netting. She smiled as she passed me by, but I doubt if she saw me. She wore a tweed suit and flat, sensible, expensive, brown shoes. The saddle as always was too low for her. Her splendid knees, one of them quite bare, rotated within easy reach of my hand: making the same motion as the knees of her father, or of any cyclist, made. But it never seemed the same.

One thing was certain: she had not flown to Belgium. Aunt Bee was wrong. Aunt Bee, as Humphrey Bogart might have said, was misinformed. Could it be that Aunt Bee was doting or just clean crazy? She talked too much about euchre and boardwalks in Atlantic City. She was old. All that whiskey. That queasy frozen soup with the bits of chicken in it. That commode which might be all very well on a battlefield, but in a civilized house in a town in Ulster, Ireland? Then another returned American had told my Uncle Owen that there was no part of the States that at some time of the year didn't get too hot, and the sun could have affected Aunt Bee's brain.

Then it dawned on me—so simply that I didn't speak about the matter for a considerable time. The shock of seeing Valerie, followed by the steep slope of Church Hill where the housewives then used to throw the dishwater out the front door into what we called the vennel—and it behoved a man to walk warily—all these may have helped to rouse me from a long dream. The first thing I saw was a Chinese junk, sail spread over a still blue pool. It was on the cover of a missionary magazine that Aunt Brigid read and kept carefully stacked up on a low wide windowsill in her house in Drumgoole. Of course it should have occurred to me to wonder how Aunt Brigid knew so much about Valerie and her people: my mother never mentioned them. But then Aunt Brigid was a travelled woman who would know about such exotics, and she could have heard it all from some knowing person in Drumgoole: and anyway I hadn't genuinely been listening, I had been thinking of Valerie on her bicycle, the maiden on her throne, boys, would be a maiden still, basket fore, basket aft, red setters trotting behind her, their tongues lolling. I had been thinking of and having my dream of fair women including the American vacationer in the Mountfield mountains, and Valerie and herself between them were, in that bemused season, all the women in the world.

So one free day Alec and myself cycled to Drumgoole and while Alec in the orchard behind the house made talk with Aunt Brigid—he was always a great man for chatting up the ladies, young and old—I had my secret consultation with the files of the magazine. There they all were in the serial story by a gentle sentimental lady novelist: old Craig and the stern Miss Meredith and even a governess called Miss Dundon, and the army officer and his friends who knew him in the squaring of his shoulders, and quite another Valerie who was known as Valerie of Elm Valley which was where she lived, somewhere in the County Cork. It was even another army. And in the latest instalment but one Valerie had run away to Belgium.

All there, and all about somebody else who had never existed except in the imagination of the novelist, and for Aunt Bee and a thousand other readers. But then never had my Valerie existed except in my imagination: and to this day I am never certain as to the degree in which Aunt Bee's mind and my own had mingled. Some of the time we may have been thinking of the same woman. There was that lost lizard blinded by a light high-up, far away and false.

In a mission-shop or Catholic Repository beside our parish church I took to buying the magazine and followed the story to its happy ending. And so we may leave Valerie. In a few days she will have changed her name. But she will always be Valerie of Elm Valley to her husband and to all those who love her.

By which time one Valerie was to me as real as the other. Once only did I speak to either of them. One day fishing along the Drumragh, at a place where the river makes a sweeping triple bend and is crossed by a decrepit but picturesque wooden footbridge, I came on a parked bicycle with two baskets, three barking but friendly red setters, and a beauty seated before an easel and painting. She asked me the name of the place. She wasn't, since she was of the garrison, too familiar with the countryside and the local names. We didn't have a lot to say to each other. She did ask me if I'd had any luck on the river and, as it happened, I hadn't. She seemed to be a practical sort of person and, in so far as I knew the difference, she painted well and she really was, as the man who looked like Rudolf Valentino said, the most beautiful woman in the world even if she was big. She was big, as the Orange song about the Sash me father wore almost says, but she was beautiful and her colours they were fine.

It was the man who looked like Valentino who years later told me that she had married into the Guards. He had kept his hair and the Valentino hairstyle. He was more courageous than another man I knew who won a prize for looking like Charles Laughton—in a prank that began as a dare in a pub—but who afterwards panicked and for the rest of his life took refuge behind a huge bushranger's beard.

—A high-ranking officer in the Coldstreams, Valentino told me. *Cor ad cor loquitur.* But then the Guards are not what they used to be, the empire's gone, pharmacy is in a decline and even the Catholic church is weak at the knees. But I saw her a year ago walking in the Haymarket in London, and she's lovelier now than she was then. She's not even so big. Women with style like that improve with the years.

As for Aunt Brigid, she finished all her whiskey and dollars and did in the end die, which was unusual for her. She was buried in a graveyard on a mountain slope three miles from Drumgoole, and in the parish where she and my mother and Owen the Lilter and the rest of them came from. And buried on the worst day God ever sent: low clouds, drizzle, and a north-east wind would skin an otter. There was a second cousin of mine at the funeral who, when she died, was on a tanker in the Persian Gulf. The company flew him back to pay his respects which was decent of the company. But he neglected to dress for the occasion and there he stood in a tropical suit, shuddering, in a church porch that was cold as a dungeon.

We took him from the churchyard gate and across the road to the public-house and bought him hot whiskey and borrowed for him a topcoat and did our best to keep the life in him. He was the coldest man I ever saw at an Irish funeral.

NEAR BANBRIDGE TOWN

THE BUFFET ON the central platform at Portadown where he changes trains always reminds him of the bridge of a ship. Unlike the bridge of a ship it is a great place for meeting people. Nobody, oddly enough, in it at the moment, but they'll come. Trains meet here, people change trains and meet. In 30 years he has passed this way more times than he can remember. Although not now for some years. Yet this very morning in a pub in Dublin at the office breaking-out Christmas party he has said, rather loudly so as to be heard above the unholy noise, that often as he has passed through Portadown, he has never once met a man who came from Portadown.

Reginald with the RAF moustache and the tweeds that will last for ever has just said that for the New Year he will give up smoking: Keep the nostrils clean, Lisney dear fellow, so as in the office to brighten the dull day by smelling the little girls.

In the bank the little girls wear not exactly a uniform, but blouses and skirts of the same colours, yellow for blouses brown for skirts. They look and smell very good. Girls from the best families get jobs in banks, and from the best schools. In the pub for the Christmas party they wear coats of many colours, drink a little more than usual and have flushed faces. Most of the men who are interested in such things know which of them do and which of them don't.

Reggie also says, as he and Lisney and Gubbins huddle in a corner as far as they can from the chaos, that in Ireland it is not commonly possible to have intercourse outside marriage. Lisney says that from his own experience he can state that that is horse-shit. Also that Gubbins here, blond and modest and three years married, has in one fortnight or fourteen days had intercourse with twelve different women not including his lady wife: three of them from the bank, one of them actually taken in the strongroom during business hours with Lisney on sentry-go to prevent interruption; two school-teachers, one fashion model, one housewife, one cinema usherette, one hotel barmaid, one college student, one lady doctor and one civil servant. Reggie admires the stamina of Gubbins and his social adaptability.

—But Gubbins, he says, you must admit that this is most unusual. You struck a pocket.

Gubbins smiles modestly but more to himself than to anybody else and goes on drinking—nourishing stout only. At this moment the six men from the Guinness ships that ferry the stuff to Liverpool come in, invading a room customarily frequented only by bank officials: but hell, it's Christmas Eve. They are big men with blue jerseys, and Guinness written in red on their chests. After a while they begin to sing very loudly: Roll out the barrel.

Reggie says, shouting to be heard: I never could stand chappies who talked shop in pubs.

In a semi-lull in the singing Lisney says that often as he has passed through Portadown he has never met a man who came from Portadown. One of the Guinness men, the biggest and most jovial and with a red moustache, says: I came from Portadown and what's more I'm not going back.

Much laughter. The Guinness men sing: Roll along, covered wagon, roll along.

The voices of the girls become more and more shrill. It is Christmas Eve in the morning. Lisney is thinking of the road ahead of him to his mother and sister in the north-west. Reggie has also recorded, on the tape-recorder in the cash-office, a rallentando of blurts prefacing it with a sennet sounded on a trumpet made from a sheet of stiff ledger paper.

The buffet is still empty except for himself and a white-coated girl behind the counter, and a stout, red-faced grey-haired, bespectacled lady, also white-coated whom, from once, often passing this way he remembers. They talk about the weather and Christmas. She says she hasn't seen him in a long time. She says the next train in won't be here for fifteen minutes. So he bites on the last of his whiskey, belts up his overcoat, says he'll walk the town for twenty minutes, ten away from the station, ten back. His own train isn't due for half an hour.

Near Banbridge town, he hums as he walks down a puddled narrow street of small brown houses, in the County Down one morning last July.

The River Bann is out there somewhere in the darkness, moving sluggishly through marsh and inert meadow, unwilling to lose itself even for a time in the big lake. Banbridge is to the south-east there and the young fellow in the song meeting on a July morning with the Star of the County Down, that sweet colleen, as she tripped down a boreen green and smiled as she passed him by. Every Ulster song should be like that one: love and love and more love and bouncing rustic beauties and none of this shit, turgid as the mud of the Bann marshes, about dying for Ireland or about King Billy on a white horse riding for ever across the River Boyne. She had a nice brown eye and a look so shy and a smile like the sun in June, and when her eye she'd roll she'd coax on me soul a spud from a hungry pig.

Holly and Christmas candles in fanlights and front windows, and here's the main street and lights and bunting for the festive season as we call it, and here's a Chinese restaurant and what did a Chinaman ever do to end up in Portadown? After the warmth of his morning's drink he could do full justice to Roseanne McCann from the banks of the Bann, she's the Star of the County Down. A spud for a hungry pig. He stops to look over a stone bridge but the water is too dark and too far away to teach him anything. No passer-by speaks to him. A dour town, a junction, he has only met one man ever who came from here and he wasn't coming back and was singing: Roll along covered wagon.

Do not use this lavatory while train is standing in station, and the wits would scribble underneath that: Except at Portadown. Yet the first man to make that joke was probably a Portadowner like all Aberdonian jokes are made by Aberdonians. He's back on the platform to the eternal smell of salt herring, and another drink and God send something in the way of amusements on the next train: She looked so sweet from her two bare feet to the crown of her nut-brown hair. Roll along covered wagon, roll along.

The buffet is still empty, even the girl with the white coat has temporarily vanished. But shadowy people are gathering on the platform around the buffet, on the two platforms across the tracks, wearily depositing parcels and suitcases, standing like statues or pacing up and down. The stout lady says that, as you would expect with the season of the year, the trains are running late. He sits on a stool and hums to himself about covered wagons and says to the stout lady: You know the street I lived on at home then led up to the co-operative creamery. It's closed now. Everything goes into a giant milk factory on the river below the town. Articulated trucks go round the country picking up the cans of milk from the farmers. But when I was a boy our road was loud and musical all morning with horse-hooves, cart-wheels, jingling silvery cans, farmboys shouting and even singing. They were great fellows for singing. There was one big chap with the biggest ears I've ever seen and a big mouth gone awry and a wet lip. The ears stuck out. He'd sit on the edge of the cart at the horse's rump, his feet trailing the ground, and sing: Rowl along discovered wagon, rowl along. To the birling of the wheels I'll sing me song. City ladies may be fine but give me Roseanne Devine, rowl along discovered wagon, rowl along. Roseanne Devine was a very bright girl, indeed, friendly with town and country. I often wondered afterwards what sort of a notion your man had of the wild west and the Oregon trail and city ladies and all that. And who in hell discovered the wagon.

The stout lady polishes glasses and listens to him patiently. The coffee cups are ready for the rush. She says: I knew Roseanne Devine. I was in the buffet in your town for two years. She was never out of the station. She met every train. She was hell for the soldiers. Somebody told me she was still alive.

—We should hope so.

He raises his glass: To Roseanne Devine and all the golden girls.

They laugh together. She's a jolly old lady. He wonders should he tell her about Reginald and Gubbins and the twelve city ladies in Dublin in fourteen days, one golden girl in the strong-room, and exclusive of the lady wife. The roar of an incoming train prevents him, which is perhaps just as well. She may not be all that jolly. As the crowd invades he retreats to a corner, secure with elbow on the counter, back to the wall, a post from which he can study the style. The white-coated girl is back and two more of the same with her. The gabble of voices, male and female, particularly female, is delightful, oh human beings were a great invention: cups rattling, steam rising, voices calling for whiskey and coffee and gin and vodka and brandy itself, it's Christmastime in Ireland and nearly everywhere else. A plaster Santa Claus, high on a bracket and up to the hips in holly, looks down on the fun.

The buffet is in two parts, one mob here, another, five paces away, over there: and looking across the two counters and between two white-coated auxiliary girls—one of them has fine shoulders —he sure as Jesus sees Lady Bob in all his glory, bright as a peacock and hasn't aged an hour since last seen ten years ago. And with him is Trooper O'Neill of the North-West Mounted Police, the Mounties always get their man. Let me, unnoticed here, just look at them, let me love them as long ago and always, let me begin with remembering the time when Trooper O'Neill and myself almost became Christian Brothers. This was how that happened. Almost happened.

Too late, though, for remembrance of things past. The trooper has spotted me and raised his right arm. Even at five paces I can't hear him with the din but I know he's shouting: Jim Lisney, Jim Lisney come over here.

Over and around he goes. It's not all that easy. But old friends are old friends and, for their sakes, barriers must be broken and strangers jostled. Glass in hand, out one door of the buffet, through the waiting—standing or pacing—shadows on the cold central platform, then in through the other door.

—Jim Lisney, Jim Lisney, says Trooper O'Neill, by God it's good to see you. Where, old sod, have you been all these years?

—Dublin.

—All those years in Dublin?

The trooper knows damned well that he has been all those years in Dublin, but what do old friends say to each other when, after long severance, they come together again? The trooper still parts his hair up the middle as he did long ago in honour and admiration of Dixie Dean who was, at that time, centre-forward for Everton. The trooper, without any obvious effort, could then give you like a song the status, scoring averages, points, positions on the League table, hopes for Wembley Stadium and the English Cup, past history and prospects of every team in every division.

—Home for Christmas, Jim? God, we'll have a great time. The old days. What are you drinking, man?

—I'm going.

—Go harder. And further. And fare better.

Reinforcements are rushed up, airborne over the heads of the first line at the counter. Lady Bob has a lime and soda.

—Crippen's dead, says Trooper O'Neill. You'll be sorry to hear.

—I heard. I must have one of the last letters he wrote.

Under a light grey overcoat, tightened at the back with a bit of a belt and a button, Lady Bob, to Lisney's amazement, is wearing a white suit. For a white Christmas. Also a blossoming pure-silk cravat. His teeth glisten. They always did. His auburn toupee might have cost hundreds. And make-up, and rings on his fingers, and bangles on his wrists, and ear-rings and a necklace. Long ago he wouldn't have dared, not even in a garrison town that was tolerant about such matters, about every matter.

—We're the commissariat, says the trooper. What would old Crippen, rest his soul, have called us?

—*Pabulatores.*

—That's it. You took the word out of my mouth. Jim, you were always a hoor for the Latin. We've two women in the guard's van.

—Hostages. Bob, I'm shocked.

—Oh, James Lisney.

A gentle smile, sweet and sad, from Bob, a bellow of laughter from the trooper: Jim, you're a hoor in your heart. The ladies are old friends. One is anyway. Sadie Crawford. Fresh from Soho. She wouldn't face out with the crowds on the platform. And the guard's van is so warm and comfy. So we're carrying back the booze and sandwiches. Give us a hand. Be with us in the van. It's the only way to travel.

—Sadie Crawford, he says, and Soho. The connection puzzles me.

But the trooper isn't listening. He has burst like a rugby forward through the ranks at the counter and is reaching back parcels and bottles to Lady Bob. When he looks around, the gold rims of his small-lensed egg-shaped spectacles positively sparkle. He is a big man bundled into a bright tweed overcoat. He is an enormous egg, dyed multi-coloured for a Gargantuan Easter and balancing on its end without aid of egg cup. Lisney moves in to help, to fetch and carry, Lady Bob isn't at his or her best in the loose scrum, even if the contiguity might be gratifying. He relays some of the provender back to Lady Bob. Around them the sound is as of the ocean, drink is being gulped down or spilled in memory of the stable of Bethlehem, angels we have heard on high sweetly singing o'er the plain. Sadie Crawford and Soho, what in the name of? But Lisney is really remembering Crippen, who is dead, and Crippen was not, needless to say, his real name.

The primary school then was a two-storeyed granite building on the top of a hill above the playground and tennis-courts and gardens and orchards; and all above the town. Stuck on to it, a three-storeyed house in which the Brothers lived and prayed and suffered. Behind it an ell-shaped modern effort of corrugated iron, lined with wooden panelling and a sort of asbestos, the secondary school, known, until it was pulled down and replaced, as the new school. The playground was vast and triangular, the base towards the town, apex pointing upwards, towards and almost reaching the two schools.

Up that triangle on a fine day in May comes, siren screaming, a police car crowded with men, some in uniform, some in plain clothes, of the local flying-squad. One lieutenant stands on one foot on the running board, prepared to leap and run into battle the moment the car slows to a moderate 50. His pistol is in his left hand, with his right he holds on to the screaming automobile.

Crippen is coming down the four steps from one of the two doors of the secondary school. He wears a pepper-and-salt tweed jacket, an open-necked white shirt and grey flannels which, as is his wont, are hoisted a little higher than is customary above his ankles. Blue socks are visible. He carries a solid brown suitcase full of the books he uses in class. His hair is closely cropped. His face is lean, suntanned, the eyes blue, boyish and excessively intelligent. He halts in dismay and attempts to run back up the steps and regain the refuge of the secondary school. Too late, alas, too late. He is surrounded at gunpoint, frisked and handcuffed. His suitcase is searched for phials of poison. Three are found. As well as Latin he also teaches chemistry. He is taken away. He doesn't struggle. The scream of the siren drops towards the heart of the town.

Nothing of this ever happened. It was all the work of the school fantasist, a man called Gordon, of infinite wit and drollery, inventor of nicknames, the more unlikely the better but with somewhere a little touch of half-zany reason in the choice. It was, anyway, a great town for nicknames and Gordon's inventions passed on from generation to generation to be used by students who never knew how or why they had been invented, or by whom.

Two of the nicknames walk there before me bearing beer and whiskey and sandwiches to two women, Sadie Crawford and A. N. Other, in the guard's van. Trooper O'Neill out of a once-popular novel of the north-west, the great lone hand, author George Goodchild. Lady Bob is quite simply Lady Bob. Apart from chemistry, which includes poisons, and a quiet demeanour, the man called Crippen had little resemblance to his great original.

There are greyhounds in the guard's van but they are, mercifully, muzzled and coralled in boxes and looking out through bars. The proper way to keep them. He has never liked greyhounds. They're not real dogs. They snap. They eat steak and drink brandy and take drugs. They lose your money. In the boxes they whine and patter on delicate feet. Sadie is not to be seen nor is the guard. But a red-headed boy sits in a wheelchair or, at any rate, he sees the back of the head of a red-headed boy, for the wheelchair, to one side of a mountain of bags and parcels, is facing the other way. Then the occupant of the machine, with a twist and a twirl, expertly wheels it around, and it isn't a boy at all but a young woman with a bony boyish face, glistening short curled hair that no treatment could ever straighten, some forehead freckles, bright blue eyes that leap out to meet the stranger and, he has to admit it near Banbridge town, she is very very beautiful. He doesn't know who she is. He can't recall anyone in his town who looked in the least like her, so that he can't have known her father or mother or aunts or uncles. She says: Sadie's in the ladies.

—That's as it should be, says the trooper. Sadie is a lady. And also this is Portadown.

And he sings: Gentlemen will please refrain from passing water while the train is stationary at the station platform.

—But ladies, he says, are different. And so is Portadown. Here, help me Jim, and Bob the Lady and Joan the Boy.

It is the only introduction they get but they are immediately and happily shoulder-to-shoulder as bottles and sandwiches and plastic glasses are laid out on a newspaper tablecloth on the top of a packing-case. Her arms are bare, the elbows dimpled. She wears denims and a white tee-shirt and written in crimson across small pointed breasts: Love my dog.

It is cosily warm in the van, happily cluttered with parcels of all shapes and sizes, Christmas parcels, a living-room in a house used by a large family when somebody has decided to tidy the place and, halfways along, given up in despair. He says: All we need is a Christmas tree.

—We have one in the corner, draped in brown paper.

Hip-bones and shoulders brush together as they help to spread the banquet.

—Welcome stranger, she says, and a happy Christmas.

It is a clear resonant voice with no accent that comes from his part of the country. She smiled as she passed me by. She is very very very beautiful. And she rolled each note from a lily-white throat.

There were two lovely girls in the town when Lisney studied under Crippen. There were many more than two but those two were particularly notable. One was called Madge and the other Dorrie. Madge had flaming red hair, was a tall, loose-limbed, overpowering girl. She was older than himself and had a regular boyfriend of her own age whom she afterwards happily married. But once he had spent two hours kissing her, or being kissed by her, in the darkness of a mild late September, on a wooden footbridge over a brawling mountain stream that came down to join the river a mile outside the town: and those two hours had been better than summer holidays and omnibus paribus, as good as anything that had ever happened to him since.

On the same evening and 40 yards away, and against a five-barred gate in another part of the happy forest, Gordon the Fantasy Man was playing fun and games with Dorrie, a small, plump brunette and very forward. One move in the games was that she snatched from his breast-pocket a Waterman fountain-pen, a present from an American uncle, which he valued more than life itself or honour even, and ran laughing a little way from him and then asked him to find the pen. Correctly he guessed where she had hidden it—Gordon was always ahead of the field and Dorrie was enticing—and lingeringly retrieved it.

She, also, was older than Gordon and had a regular boyfriend of her own age whom she afterwards happily married.

Oh, red Madge and dark Dorrie and Gordon of the Nicknames and a lost happy September, and he thinks of them now when he thinks of Crippen because one evening Dorrie said to him and Trooper O'Neill and Gordon and the Dead Man McCartney, so-called because he looked like Buster Keaton, that Crippen would be the handsomest man in the town if he would only let his trousers down.

Much coarse laughter and Dorrie even blushed.

She meant merely that he should relax his gallases, braces or suspenders, and cover his ankles. He was, indeed, a very handsome man, clean, clean-living, clean-spoken, just and fair to all mankind, learned and capable of passing on some little of his learning to others: and not in the least like the sad Englishman who dosed the wife and was captured by cable. He lived and died a bachelor and was not thus exposed to the temptations that bedevilled his namesake.

The train is under way. Sadie has returned. She is as brilliant as Lady Bob who in the warmth of the guard's van has taken off his overcoat, folded it carefully, placed it on newspaper on top of one of the barred wooden cells which encloses a malevolent-looking black bitch. No guard is yet to be seen. In a remote corner of the van and behind a mountain-range of parcels two young rug-headed fellows in brown coats are sipping glasses of stout and sorting letters into a rack.

Lady Bob, overcoatless, is now seen to wear, like a matador, a black silk bellyband holding in place, if they need any holding, those skint-tight white pants. Cravatless, and the cravat is laid to rest on top of the overcoat, he displays a short-sleeved tartan shirt, with low, curved not pointed, cleavage, and a smooth white chest, hairless by nature or depilation. Praised be to the Lord of Hosts, but my town has never looked back since the day when, as Gordon used to say, one of the Lyons married into the English royal family. For there was then in the town a clan that went by the name of Lyon, and the old people, who should know about such things, used to say that there were always five generations of the Lyons living at the same time. So to Sadie, by way of greeting and after some years, he says: Who won the war?

And embraces her and kisses both her powdered cheeks.

And Sadie answers: Who but the Lyons?

For a stroller in the dark, on lovers' lanes around the town and in the years between the two wars, might for no reason except hellery or the love of life cry out that question, and be thus answered by some other anonymous voice. To Joan the Boy, Sadie explains: There were so many of them, you see, in the British army and once on a time at the western front. We used to say they won the war. Trust you to remember that, Jim Lisney.

—Old Jamie, the great-grandfather was, they said, in the house in an armchair, stuffed. Your brother, Mick, told me that.

—But once a week, Jim Lisney, he was allowed up and out to walk the greyhounds.

In the noisy swaying van they hold on to each other and laugh at the fantasy, and Lisney nibbles her ear and is conscious that though she has passed 50, her waist and hips are as firm as good rubber. She wears a wine-coloured blazer with white military-style piping. And a dark blue shirt with tartan top, not a blouse. And carries a white plastic shopping-bag ornamented with an enormous brimstone butterfly, also plastic. She has jet-black bobbed hair in memory of Jessie Mathews or Claudette Colbert or somebody, and a wide red mouth and large gentle brown eyes like the Star of the County Down, and a mole with two hairs to the left of her mouth. The singer of the love song said nothing about moles. And a smile like the sun in June.

—And one day Freddy Lyon let me look at the ferret he used to catch all the rabbits with.

When the trap was opened it came out of the dirty wooden box, itself coloured a dirty cream that was almost grey, sinuous as a snake and like a snake, also, in that it didn't seem to have legs or even feet. Not a ferret but a stoat—we don't have true ferrets in Ireland—and we called this monster by the odd name of whitthrit. It looked at nobody. It flowed and looped around again and went back into the box, and Freddy dropped the trap. He said: Nothing here for him to do on that bare ground. They're very intelligent.

He was sitting on the mounting-block, used no longer, never to be used again, at the corner of the smithy, at the entrance to the Back Alley. A thin cadaverous man, never quite shaven, shabby grey jacket, peaked cap, a quite incongruous pair of professorial horn-rimmed spectacles: and very gentle. He had soldiered for a while but the health caught up on him. He hunted with his friend, the ferret, genuinely his friend, they understood each other. Expertly he fished the rivers and lakes, pitying the fish, but food was food. Then he died. He could at times be a philosopher. One day, seated on the mounting block, hands joined, fingers knit between his knees, he said: Jim Lisney, if you don't eat you starve, if you don't shite you bust.

He tells this to Sadie and to Trooper O'Neill but only to them. Screams and roars of laughter in the rocking guard's van. Lady Bob and Joan the Boy are spreading the repast on a shiny blue trunk belonging to somebody who is travelling in more orthodox fashion. Sadie says: The day of Freddy's funeral I was coming out of the church behind two old dames from Fountain Lane. All glorious in black shawls. And scattering holy water over each other. And one of them says, Jesus knows, Maggie, that's the first of the Lyons ever died.

A bellow from Trooper O'Neill, red-coated hero of the white, north-west, the Mounties always get their man. From behind a tree Nelson Eddy bellows: When I'm calling you, hoo-hoo-hoo, hoo-hoo-hoo-hoohoo. The boom of the train means that they are going through a tunnel, there's only one on this line, or under a long long bridge of which there are several, going home for a holy Christmas, burrowing deeply into the brown earth that nourished them. A poet he knows in Dublin, a big, gentle, uncouth, splay-footed man touched by God, tells him how he went home for last Christmas, a drink here, a drink there, several (he said several) drinks at Amiens Street Station, seven drinks with old friends at Dundalk, nine drinks with older friends in the roadside pub by oil-lamplight at Blackhorse Halt, then out along the lonely road, suitcase in hand, running at the hills like a horse that knows he's nearing home, like a horse, he said.

The beauty of the guard's van is that you're not haunted by reflections from any windows, ghosts, including your own, travelling with you, bending forwards, leaning back, talking without sound, gesturing, mocking, mimicking. The van is a sealed refuge, a little world apart.

—In that family, Lisney remembers, they had a slew of grand-fathers. They had to have or they couldn't all have been there. When I was ten I played street football with Jack and Jimmy Lyon, two little leprechauns even for their age. One day it rained. And Jack and Jimmy said: We'd bring you into the house to play only our oul granda's in and he's crabbed.

—We peeped in through a kitchen window and there he was, a wee man with a beard and a stick, hunched in a low armchair, smoking and spitting.

The trooper says that there was one of the same in every house the Lyons lived in.

The preliminary bombardment eases. Through drifting smoke, with bayonets threatening, a thousand Lyons, little boys and pallid hunters and bearded spitting grandsires with sticks, advance to beat the Germans. These all were part of the furniture of my boyhood. Mons, Mons, Mons, the word keeps ringing like a bell.

—And one day, Sadie, I saw Jack and Jimmy take money out of their mother's purse. To steal money from your mother, I thought, was a bad thing.

—Since then, Jim Lisney, I'd say that you've taken a lot that didn't belong to you or your mother.

—Hoo—hoo—hoo. Hoo—hoo—hoo—hoo—hoo—hoohoo.

—But I'd no scruple helping to eat the proceeds when he spent it in Hop McConnell's sweetie shop.

—My dear father, says Lady Bob.

And Lisney is momentarily but not seriously embarrassed by remembering that Hop McConnell was, indeed, the dear father of Lady Bob, and always a little inclined, as he hopped, to wonder about the son that he and his sainted, slender, Bible-reading wife had brought into the world.

—It was Gordon made us all laugh, Sadie says, when Miss Bowes-Lyon, a commoner, married King George. He said the Lyons were getting up in the world.

It was Gordon said this and Gordon said that and then Gordon is with them in the guard's van, is, in fact, the guard and Lisney is

again embarrassed because he should have remembered that after
the war Gordon took a job on the railways. We cut the links that
bind us or they rust and snap of their own accord. People live on in
our memory as they once were. We forget they are living differently
now, other times, other places. We even forget that they are
dead.

Sleep and philosophy and Christmas Eve are overtaking me.

But Gordon's handgrip is strong and friendly and reassuring.
Hands don't change. He says: Jim Lisney, I thought you knew.

The clean-cut face is the same, the sharp exact words. Lisney
says that he did know, he had heard: But then I got mixed-up,
began to think you never came home again.

—Thinking all the time of himself, Sadie says. He hasn't come
up from Dublin in years.

—No Jim, Gordon says, it was Dead Man McCartney never
came home. Joined the Palestine police. Went East after that and
married a Chinawoman. Lucky man.

Sadie says that it's not true, that Anna May Wong said so. They
laugh, even Joan the Boy and Lady Bob, at the hoary joke. They sit
to eat and drink. There are two low stools and two tip-up seats on
the side of the van, and several boxes, and the two rug-headed
stout-sipping sorters join them. Joan the Boy sits down on Gordon's left knee. To Lisney's slight annoyance. Now, as then, Gordon has the way with him, and Gordon, further to increase the
annoyance, says: The other knee, Tilly daughter.

She changes her seat to the right knee. Gordon explains: You
could sit all night on that knee and it would do nothing for me. Or
you. I think.

And Lisney remembers that he had heard that Gordon had lost
a leg. He says: Tilly?

She asks him: What is it, stranger?

—Joan?

—Tilly's my name, dear handsome stranger.

Sadie says: She acted in a play. In armour and a sword. A girl
would need them nowadays.

Gordon asks: In Soho, Sadie?

—Anywhere. With the likes of you and Jim Lisney groping around.

Gordon's right hand is gently stroking a thigh of Joan the Boy. Lisney is no longer glad to see Gordon again and also he knows now where he saw the Boy before, except that it wasn't her but Siobhán MacKenna or some lesser actress, young lambs crying across the healthy frost, Joan the Boy, for two hours he kissed Madge but down the road, Gordon, ahead of the field, was lingeringly discovering where Dorrie had hidden the fountain-pen and the sandwiches taste like chalk as he studies the pressure of that neat rump on Gordon's living knee, and Gordon asks: Where's the Tec.?

On the authority of the trooper it would seem that the Tec., whoever he is, has met an old friend up the train and is now in the bar and will be along later to sing Noël, Noël, and Christmas Day in the morning: and the long, long booming of the train now certainly indicates that they are in the line's one tunnel and above them in the night is the humped, clenched, sectarian bitterness of Dungannon town.

The trooper excuses himself, gulps the tail-end of a drink and temporarily withdraws.

The two rug-headed sorters return to their rack and refill their stout-glasses. They are silent young men. The train, clear of the tunnel and somewhere on high dark moorland, rattles like castanets. Joan the Boy dismounts from Gordon's knee, the hoyden saint descending from her charger, and sits on one of the tip-up seats. Lady Bob, shivering slightly at the brief sudden draught when the trooper opens the corridor door, rises, restores his overcoat. Sadie on a box cushioned by mail-bags leans back against a larger box, stretches arms and legs, belches, and doesn't bother to excuse herself. They are warm and relaxed and happy and Sadie sings that Christmas is coming and the geese are getting fat, so please put a penny in the poor man's hat. Very quietly the Boy says that Christmas is here.

—A bit sad for you this year Tilly, says Sadie.

And explains to Lisney that the Boy has had a bereavement in the family. He is sorry to hear it but the Boy says that it was only a grandmother and she was as old as sin and grandmothers are sort of expected to die, even if you were very attached to them as she was to this one. So she's back from London for the funeral. Lisney wonders again about Sadie and Soho, but it doesn't seem to be the time to mention any place so remote as the idea or image of Soho is, from the memory of dear dead grandmothers. In the warm silence that follows they grow closer together. Now that the Boy is safely in the saddle on the tip-up seat and away from the threat of the living leg, Lisney finds that his old affection for Gordon is restored: how, anyway, could you hide a fountain-pen in those tight denims? Out of the past he remembers to himself this and that. But it is Gordon who touches the telepathic chord.

—The trooper, he says. Do you remember, Jim, the time the trooper and yourself were going to become Christian Brothers? Being a Protestant, Tilly, you wouldn't know much about things like this.

—I was St Joan.

—She was a class of a Protestant. They burned her, didn't they? But the way it was when we were beginning secondary school, the recruiting officer used to come around.

—For the army?

—No, Tilly. I knew you wouldn't get it. For the Christian Brothers. A smiling elderly brother, seemed elderly to us, from the Headhouse in Dublin.

—The Headhouse? The Nuthouse?

—The Mother House, Tilly.

—Were they mothers or brothers?

—Dear sweetheart, just listen.

Lisney is annoyed again, well at least uneasy.

—This brother would gather around him all the guys between twelve and fifteen and give them a little talk about Jesus.

—His birthday's tomorrow. Even if I'm a Protestant I heard about him.

—So did Joan.

—She heard voices, Gordon.

—Listen Tilly, just listen to my voice, one voice only. Talk to them about Jesus and ask them what they wanted to do with their future life.

—Did any of you ever tell him? Did any of you guess right?

—The way he went about it was to ask us to write an essay, paragraph, half a page. Lisney wrote a great one. Do you recall? To carry the standard of Christ among the peoples of darkest Africa.

—Were you crazy?

She's asking Lisney.

—No, the game was that if you came up with one like that it made life easier. It worked, too. Saved my life once in a Latin class when I was called out, the axe about to descend for work not done, for an interview, the recruiting officer had turned up again for his annual visit, wanted to see how fared the apostle of Africa.

—Hypocrisy, she says. Jim. And Gordon, what did you say you wanted to be?

—A one-legged guard on a railway train. One fellow whose father was a doctor said he wanted to be a butcher. He didn't like his father. He got jail later on for stealing a car and blowing up a customs hut on behalf of the IRA.

—And the trooper?

—A Christian Brother, Lisney says. Just like that. He was straightforward.

—Did he want to?

—Not on your life. The trooper was an expert on the soccer results. We were destined, as they put it, for the English mission. The novitiate was in Liverpool. The trooper said to me: Lisney lad, every second Saturday we'll be able to see Everton playing at home. Dixie Dean, Coulter, Stevenson, Alec Cook the full-back.

—None of you ever became.

—Look around and see, Sadie says. They became something all right. What did you really say, Gordon? In the composition.

—A British soldier, Sadie. Like my father before me. The Dead Man, wrote a sailor. He became that too. Our dreams came true.

—So there you are, says Trooper O'Neill, working moves. Watch out, Sadie. Watch out, Joan.

Heat or no heat he has not unburdened himself of the egg-shaped tweed and there's a faint dew on his high narrow forehead. The Tec. is with him, a small quick-stepping man with a brown hat, a brown moustache, a white rubbery trench-coat: and Lisney remembers the Tec. and the Tec. remembers him. It was years ago, they agree, at Portadown station, and the Tec. explains: You and the man with you were talking Irish. That was why the sergeant, the constable and myself questioned you.

—We were talking Irish to rise you.

—Likely. It wasn't very good Irish. I was born in Connemara and spoke it from the cradle. But the previous day a constable had been shot dead at Dungannon and in this part of Ireland he was more likely to be shot dead by somebody who spoke bad Irish. So we questioned you.

—Quiet times now, Lisney says.

But Sadie, rising to pour drinks, says that the times will be worse before they're better, that when the marching begins the trouble begins but, for God's sake, with Christmas on top of them they've better things to do than talk about politics and, anyway, the tec. is retired now and going away to live in the west of Ireland where he came from and, as well, Jim Lisney was never interested, that she had heard, in anything except women and that, if it hadn't been for the wolfhound by her side he'd have twitched the green gown off Mother Erin herself, and he with one on him like a round tower.

—Oh Sadie dear, says Lady Bob.

They all laugh except Joan the Boy who is stooped tidying-up in the corner of the van and very well she looks in that position.

Then from a newspaper that he has carried with him from Dublin, Lisney reads out that a stallion in a stud-farm in Kildare has got 6,000 guineas for one performance, all that and money too, and that a married woman in England says that a tall dark stranger bewitched his way into her bed, and bewitched her out of £1,100.

—Sadie, he says, I've wasted my golden youth.

I'll follow you, Gordon says, to the First and the Last.

He limps away. He says to Lady Bob: I nicknamed your father Hop, and now I'm hopping myself.

—Dear Gordon, says Lady Bob. My father loved you.

And runs a few paces after Gordon and embraces him: But darling I won't go to the First and the Last. It's so rough and crowded.

—But Bob I thought you liked it rough and crowded. Fifi, Bobby or any name will do.

Lower lips pouting in a parody of Maurice Chevalier, Gordon pinches a cheek and holds on and Bob squeals with delight and goes with the others to the First and the Last: leading the way with the trooper, and Joan the Boy between them, and Sadie and Lisney twenty paces behind. Parcels have appeared like seagulls over a homecoming trawler and the five of them are clumsily burdened, the tec. has gone on to Derry city: and Sadie drops a parcel, and Lisney and herself, stooping together to pick it up, bump skulls as people always do, and laugh and retrieve the parcel and straighten up again, and look ahead under a railway bridge to where the lighted doors of the First and the Last are closing behind the other three. Beyond that, there's a row of white cottages and diminishing street lamps and then the brooding darkness of divided rural Ulster: the town and its life and lights behind them.

—She's a lovely young girl, Sadie says. Treat her well, Jim Lisney.

—I'll buy her all the drink in the house.

—Quite well you know what I mean. She has an eye for you.

—She sat on Gordon's knee.

—Gordon's an uncle to her.

—Uncles can be odd.

—Or a much older brother. Anyway Gordon gave it all up long ago. He married an Englishwoman. Strict. And anyway they're still in love. The wife I mean. And Gordon. She's a fine young one, Tilly I mean, out of the ordinary.

—She is Joan the Boy, Sadie. She doesn't look like a Tilly. She is an able-bodied country-girl of seventeen or eighteen, respectably dressed in red——

—You're colour-blind. Or you're mad. And she was born in Darlington, England.

—With an uncommon face——

—She has an angel's face. Keep it that way, Jim Lisney, you grey-headed bastard. To think that you used to look like Gregory Peck except they say he's a good man. Villainy shows in the end. Too many wrinkles too soon and your face as grey as your hair.

—Her eyes are very wide apart and bulging as they often do in very imaginative people. She has a full-lipped mouth and a handsome fighting chin.

—Why did you say bulging eyes? What's all that about?

—Sadie, it's all in the play. My other name is Ladvenu.

—It's Lad Something, sure enough.

—It was Ladvenu in the play.

—What play?

—The play that Joan was burned in.

—That play didn't mean much to me. Not a laugh in it from start to finish. A dangerous play. All talk. Because Tilly was in it I saw it. But I didn't see you.

—Not the same performance, Sadie girl. My play was in Dublin. The bank official's musical and dramatic society.

—Oh la-dee-da. And you were lad—ee—da.

—Ladvenu, a decent young Dominican friar.

—Christ graciously hear us. You?

—Ladvenu was all for Joan. He took pity on her. He tried to save her from the burning.

—If he was anything to you he wanted to keep her for himself. No offence though, Jim, you always had a bit of a name for the girls. But you weren't the worst, nobody ever found out who was the worst. My brothers were all for you, they said you were the best boy ever to read poetry in the room behind the shop.

He is fascinated by Sadie's hair, spotlighted, as they advance, by a streetlight. It shines so as to dazzle, almost. From much association with women in the bank but, unlike Gubbins, not that way on the sacred premises and certainly not in the strong-room, he knows that her hair has had henna treatment with a sort of wax that the women, or the teevee ads, say gives a gloss, shiny and healthy, the way a thoroughbred would look when well-groomed and curry-combed, or whatever they do to placate and make more perfect four-legged gentlemen who can earn £6,000 by one act of pleasure: and the elder of Sadie's two brothers is running naked up and down a summery riverbank beating his chest with his fists and making noises like Tarzan. Six or so female nurses from the mental hospital are high on a stone bridge that carries the Belfast railway over the river—we crossed it twenty minutes ago. The nurses are laughing so as to be heard by all the men and boys splashing in the river, sunning on the bank.

—They know, Gordon says, that they'll get him in the end if he goes on much longer the way he's going.

He must have been one of the hairiest men in the world, all black and bristling except for his head which was bald and shining white. To get to that cool pool on the river you had to walk two miles along the railway track. By the time you had walked home again to the town on a hot summer day you needed another cold swim. Here and now on Christmas Eve I can smell the tar and the timber of the sleepers, hear the crunch of a careless foot on the ballast, smell the deep warm grass on embankments and cuttings, safe shelters for lovers. That pool was a heavenly place, an all-male heaven, no woman's eye ever looked down on it except those eyes of the strong laughing nurses from the mental which was half a mile downstream. An uproariously funny place, too, and Sadie's brother, the elder of the two, the best part of the fun: hairy body, bald head, horn-rimmed spectacles as big as bicycle lamps, doing his Tarzan act, leaps and runs and somersaults and cartwheels and high yodelling calls for the benefit of the ladies on the bridge. Who did get him in the end but only for a few months out of every year.

—When he's in, Gordon said, the other's out. To run the shop. It's a foolproof system. Lunatic-proof.

But mostly the two of them were out together, running the shop and the wholesale business, at night presiding over a parliament of a dozen or so pals around the range in the kitchen behind the shop, drinking porter, playing twenty-five, reading out loud from the papers, and even poetry by God, or having it read to them like lords and princes in castles and old walled towns: Stand up there, young Lisney, and read out that. Prove to us that your da isn't throwing away good money sending you to school.

Mostly it was Dangerous Dan McGrew and a bunch of the boys were whooping it up in the Malamute saloon, were you ever out in the Great Alone when the moon was awful clear, with only the howl of a timber wolf and you camped out there in the cold, clean mad for the muck called gold, and that night on the marge of Lake Labarge I cremated Sam McGee, and Sadie coming and going, hair then flying and not lacquered down, mostly I remember her in a red dress, moving somnolent boozers or absorbed gamblers out of her way just for the womanly hell of it, and saying to him now: Jim Lisney, are you listening to me at all?

They are standing facing each other and still 30 or so paces from the door of the First and the Last. It's a corner house. It booms, it reverberates, the walls bulge with Christmas merriment. He asks Sadie: Have you gazed on naked grandeur when there's nothing else to gaze on . . .?

—So that's the way your mind's moving.

—Have you known the great White Silence, not a snow-gemmed twig a-quiver? What's this I hear about Sadie and Soho?

Then he is back and Sadie with him in the bedlam, Bethlehem by Jesus, of the morning, all over the world (almost) men are toasting the King of Peace. Toasting him bloody-well brown. In a corner under brown bellying barrels a group of raucous men and demented women are singing out that auld acquaintance should na be forgot, that memories should be brought to mind: and what has he been at every minute since he stood on the bridge of the ship at Portadown, and seeing memories come presently alive before him, and out there in the great dark silence is the brooding countryside, candles of Christmas peace lighted in many windows: and in there is the crowded town his mother and sister are readying the

house for the prodigal's homecoming, for auld lang syne, and
Sadie, close to him in the crowd, booze and perfume, kohl pencil
melting in the heat around serious· protruding eyes, has a statement to make about Soho: I'm dead serious Jim Lisney, dead
serious now, listen to me.

With Sadie he had waltzed while she sang the Merry Widow and
remembered Maurice Chevalier and Jeannette MacDonald until
Gordon cut in and brought the house down as he whirled, using his
stiff leg to describe a perfect circle. Above the foot of the bed the
Queen of England, busby and red jacket, sits on a black horse and
pretends not to see them. She has a nice blue eye and a look so shy
and, in the small hours and between the sheets and under the
queen, she is surprisingly gentle, the tigrish look of youth gone, a
gentle face, the resting face of a young mother. She'd coax, upon
me soul, a spud from a hungry pig. She says that he is to do her no
harm and he tells her that that is not what he came all this way for,
all the way back to where he came from: To think that when I saw
you first in the van, in the wheelchair, I thought you might be a
cripple.
    —Would you have loved me less? Or more?
    —Can't do any better than I'm doing.
    No horse I'll yoke, no corn I'll cut, no sod with the plough turn
down——
    —What was your nickname?
    —. . . till smiling bright by my own fireside sits the Star of the
County Down.
    —Skinny.
    —Were you? You're not now.
    —Not that skinny. But Skinny Lisney. You see. Skinny Lizzie.
Subtle.
    Then after a lull he says: The queen's horse has whinnied.
    —That was no horse. That was me.
    And when her breath returns she says: Happy Christmas.
    And: What was Gordon's nickname?
    —He never really had one. But I called him Sir Gordon. He rode

so many winners. Gordon Richards, you know, the famous jockey.
Sir Gordon.

—From now on I'll call him Sir Gordon.

Is he uneasy again? Not that it really matters. The world is for
his wishing. Cold Christmas morning is outside the window. This
he knows is their first and last meeting.

—I feel like Nero.

—That's better than Gordon. I'll call you Nero.

His suitcase has been left in the First and the Last and the only
luggage he has taken away with him is a bottle of Power's Gold
Label, his mother now and then likes a nip in hot milk at bedtime,
in a stainless-steel tankard, with a spoonful of honey added to
catch the secret of the sun. The bottle, splendid with its golden
shield, stands on a tallboy by the bedroom window. Tallboy's a
funny word. Together they laugh over it. The tip of her tongue is a
butterfly. Next time round she lies back laughing and says that
Sadie, since she first heard the going rate in Soho, says that no girl
should do all that for nothing, that the girls in Soho make a mint or
a mink, that Sadie will get herself arrested preaching that message
all over the town.

—I'm dead serious, Jim Lisney, dead serious, now listen to me.

—What's that squeaky noise?

—That was Sadie. Preaching to me. Last night.

—You're no mimic, no actor.

—I was Ladvenu,

—I'll call you Ladvenu. My voices have deceived me. I have
been mocked by devils: my faith is broken. I have dared and dared:
but only a fool will walk into a fire.

—My lord: what she says is, God knows, very wrong and shock-
ing: but there is a grain of worldly sense in it such as might impose
on a simple village maiden.

—Ladvenu, that's Sadie you're talking about. She didn't ask you
to strike a rate for making love. Surely to God. Or arbitrate?

—Like the Labour Court in Dublin.

—Labour's a four-letter word.

—Dead serious, Jim Lisney. You talk about wasting your golden youth. Think of all the time the girls in this town waste, misused, abused, manhandled, against five-barred gates, in the corners of fields and the backs of cars, in haystacks, the marks of the iron bars on their backsides forever, hayseed in the hair and not a penny to show for it. Every man, my motto is, should be compelled to pay his way or face a strike. Down tools, Sadie, I said. Jim Lisney, jokes apart, pack up I tell them and head for Soho.

Laugh as much as we may at Sadie, the queen, who sometimes lives quite close to Soho, refused to laugh with us. On the wall beyond the tallboy and beside a wardrobe is a coloured picture-poster of a young girl, round-faced, smiling naked and normal except that a mirror is inset to her middle to give the oddest effect of pain, distortion, screaming.

—The queen up there, he says, on her high horse.

—What about her?

—She's not looking at us.

—Would you expect her to?

—The girl? With the glass belly.

—That's me. My image of me.

—Fragile. This end up. Is this your bedroom?

—They keep it for me.

—They?

—They've gone on to the funeral. I'll follow.

—What does Gordon mean to you?

—We're just good friends. Like film stars. Or yourself and Gordon.

—But we're old friends, boyhood friends, and we're two men.

Cuddling, teasing, no longer Joan the Boy, she asks him is he jealous. He isn't. Or is he? And if so, for what reason? This here, on the bed under the inattentive horse-borne queen, will be the first and the last meeting, and if Gordon has also been here would that not be the real reunion of friends, Madge and Dorrie by the bridge over the mountain stream, this journey to the most secret places, this communion at Christmas, the feast of friends, the candle-fruited tree.

She is asleep again, curled up like a child, turned towards me, hands, very small hands, clutching or resting on my right shoulder, mouth a little open, breathing very lightly. The clock in the far corner ticks away the seconds towards the time when I must leave her and go through the cold empty town and face up to a sorrowful mother and hostile sister in what was once my home, though never quite my home for they moved to a new house after my father died and long after I left the town. The clock ticks away, an answering ticking from the corner behind me, except that if I crush my left ear on the pillow the answering ticking no longer answers. An echo, or the ghost of a clock that may have been there when she was younger or when somebody else who may now be dead slept in this room? An uncanny effect: left ear off the pillow and two clocks tick, muffle the left dear and one clock stops, clocks stop in rooms when people die, she sleeps on.

Then watching her opening eyes he sings softly: Oh, I wish the Queen of England would write to me in time and place me in some regiment all in my youth and prime. . . .

—You'd be left with one leg, like Gordon.

—Gordon, Gordon.

—You can't take your eyes off the queen. Look at me instead.

—I'm looking.

—We were loyal Ulster Protestants. That's why she's up there in all her glory, like Joan herself, riding on a horse. I was a brownie, and a girl-guide all dressed in blue, salute to the king, bow to the queen and now I must go to the bathroom.

He lies alone, his eyes closed, wishing he could lie there forever, dreading the cold outside, the frost, the sorrow ahead to which he has contributed his share, the hostility which, perhaps, he helped to create. He remembers on holiday, when he was fourteen, in the town of Enniskillen, the wide waters of the Erne opening out around it, the deep deep meadows and continual corncrakes, most of his time spent bait-fishing for perch and bream under the hill topped by Portora Royal School where Oscar Wilde had been as a boy: deep lake water, lazy days, perch in plenty until Hetty came along and he lost interest in fish and lay with her in the sunny corner behind an abandoned boathouse, Hetty, Hetty, Hetty, a quiet, tall pale-faced girl, the second name has gone for ever: and when he touched her there, just there, she winced and drew her legs together with the strength of a vice and he was staggered to discover that Protestant girls had the same reactions as Catholic girls. Because they didn't have to go to confession they were supposed to be free as the wind and easy. Hetty, Hetty, Hetty, he says it out loud he is trying so hard to recall that lost surname: and she is back in the room and kneeling naked by a record-player on the floor at the feet of the girl with the glass belly, and Kathleen Ferrier, who died too young from cancer, is filling Christmas with her splendid voice, singing that she has a bonnet trimmed with blue and that now sleeps the crimson petal of the rose, and singing about the stuttering lover and about the fair house of joy to which fond love hath charmed me and, this is it and here it is, he says.

She snuggles. She says: Ladvenu, it's cold outside.

And: Who is Hetty?

—It's who was Hetty. It's a long time ago.

He tells her: And what amazed me, as I tell you, was that she winced and she a Protestant when I touched her there, just there.

—Here's one Protestant girl that will neither wince nor twice nor thrice. How do you say four that way?

—I'd try four times.

—Why not, and five or six or seven if you're fit.

No horse I'll yoke, no corn I'll cut, no sod with the plough turn down. Begod says I to a passer-by who's the maid with the nut-brown hair. She'd coax on me soul a spud from a hungry pig when her eyes she'd roll. That was no horse, that was me. Till smiling bright by my own fireside, sorrowful mother and hostile sister, fair house of joy to which fond love hath charmed me: and wince, she says, and twice and thrice and frice and fice and sice and seven-up sits the Star of the County Down.

There is an old stone bridge over the river, wide and shallow at that point, and right in the middle of the town. On a mellow spring evening he is leaning on the mossy parapet. He is alone. At that

moment there is no crossing traffic, none at all. Crippen has
become a member of the town council. He wants to beautify the
place. In class he talks of amenities, environment, ecology and how
every town that has a fine river should have a fine river-walk. From
the bridge Lisney looks down at the sun, a perfect undisturbed
circular reflection, unquivering, standing quite still although the
shallows rattle all around it. He looks down also on a sort of mossy
stone shelf where Crippen has planned the beginning of the river-
walk. Above the shelf rise high garden walls, grey stone, red brick
and brown, and above them a steep slope, gardens and orchards:
higher still the backs of the houses of the High Street: three church
spires over all. To his left—the parapet runs right into it—is a high
house where a man made harness and saddles and also distilled
poteen, right in the heart of the town, right under the noses of the
police, a quarrelsome man, an old crusty bachelor with a quarrelsome nephew, a young crusty bachelor: and one day, making
saddles and sampling their own poteen, the two of them had a
set-to that rocked the town, and the nephew went off in fury to
another town and, drunk in a pub, told a stranger how his bastard
of an uncle was still clever enough to make poteen in the heart of a
town and right under the noses of the police. The stranger was a
policeman in plain clothes who reached for the 'phone and rang the
other policemen to tell them about what was under their noses.
The saddler, when he heard them beating on the door, ran the
poteen into the river down that black rainspout and it was said that
every fish for ten miles downstream was drunk and singing: but the
worm and the still he couldn't run down the spout and a good trade
was ruined: Lisney looks at the black downspout and wonders how
it is that while he is standing on the bridge he knows that Joan the
Boy is sleeping beside him, fair house of joy. But on the mossy
stony shelf a mother and child are walking, laughing, talking
German, he can hear them quite clearly. Then the child falls into
the shallow water but continues to laugh and talk German and is
kicking about and splashing in high delight. That river-walk never
got to any distance. The effluent from a piggery came out over it
just down there. The pigman was a power on the town council.

Crippen wasn't even a native townsman. Gordon concocted epics about the war of Crippen and the pigman, and the poisoning of the pigs by Crippen, and the drowning of Crippen by the pigman in deep pools of slurry: and Lisney runs to help the German mother to get the child out of the river. He leaves his suitcase on the sidewalk on the bridge. When he comes back one of a crowd of passing schoolboys—they have come out of nowhere, like screaming, swooping gulls—is about to steal the case. He apprehends him, lectures him, forgives him because the boy is himself, but when the boy has gone out of sight he realizes that it isn't his case at all but an abrased battered thing with nothing in it but one boot, a few tattered books, some rusted cutlery, a pair of female underpants, raggedy. So to the still sun in the shallow river he screams and curses about why does he ever carry anything about with him, that he's always losing things everywhere, all his life long, that life is one long process of loss and attrition until life itself is also lost or worn away: and then he is saying all that to an American friend in the lobby of an hotel in New York, that he is always losing things, always leaving things behind him in hotels, and the friend says that New York claims no credit for the loss of his virginity which was on another battlefield and faraway. Yet he knows that she is there beside him and he struggles to awake and does awake in a room in that same hotel in New York, the 'phone ringing and the voice of a Mr Runciman enquiring for a M. Ladvenu Lisney who has survived an air disaster in Monte Video. He sees that he is in the wrong room. The floor is littered with women's shoes. The wardrobe is stuffed with perfumed clothes of blinding colours. His wife, Madame Lisney, comes into the room. She doesn't recognize him. Joan the Boy is standing by the window stepping into and hooking herself into her underclothes, behind her the naked girl with the glass belly, the tension, the screaming, the pain. Joan tells him that it's frosty outside, Ladvenu, that it looks like a hard north-east wind, that he's not to move, that she'll make some breakfast, that there are five magpies teasing a cat in a pear tree, he can hear their wicked screams of mockery, that what would he like for breakfast, that for herself she can often be content with bread and coffee, that it is no hardship to drink coffee if the coffee be Nescafé: but to shut me from the light of the sky and the sight of the fields and flowers: to chain my feet so that I can never again ride with the soldiers nor climb the hills: to make me breathe foul damp darkness, and keep from me everything that brings me back to the love of God when your wickedness and foolishness tempt me to hate him: all this is worse than the furnace in the Bible that was heated seven times. I could do without my warhorse: I could drag about in a skirt———

She zippers the fly of her crumpled denims, the magpies give one fearful orchestrated scream and fly away and leave the cat to a cold frustrated Christmas around a house that will soon be empty.

—I could let the banners and the trumpets and the knights and soldiers pass me and leave me behind as they leave the other women, if only I could still hear the wind in the trees, the larks in the sunshine, the young lambs crying through the healthy frost, and the blessed blessed church bells that send my angel voices floating to me on the wind . . . Coffee for Ladvenu.

The bells are indeed ringing. Seven-thirty. The morning angelus. The angel of the Lord declared unto Mary and she conceived of the Holy Ghost. His third awakening this morning, and out of the dream of the fair house of joy, will be down there in the frosty, misty valley, in the empty streets.

He steps out into the north-east wind which wakes the sleeping rheum and graces the parting with many tears, and knows where he is or, rather, has his bearings, knows what part of the town he's in, knows the way to go home. This road once was well out on the fringe of the town, clean cottages standing on half-acres, flowers and apple trees and black and red-currant bushes: cottages built for ex-soldiers, the queen might have ridden on many a wall, not seeing many a sight. Very much built up now, blocks of new two-storeyed houses have swamped the cottages, eaten into the gardens. He is quite alone on Christmas morning. The angel of the Lord, the bells said, had declared unto Mary but the bells had not yet said come all to church, good people, good people come and pray. She had given him a Christmas cake to make up for his missing luggage and to go with the whiskey: they wouldn't need the cake at the funeral, he could say he'd left the suitcase on the train.

Over to his left and behind a phalanx of new houses he sees the outline of the Quarries, magnified by the half-light and the frosty mist into Gothic cliffs. Long ago worked-out and abandoned to wilderness and secret lovers. All the wild thoughts and talk that place used to provoke when Gordon and himself, the trooper and the Dead Man and the Dead Man's dog would go rabbiting there on fine mornings and study the traces of the night before: damp crushed mattresses of newspapers in trenches under bushes and briars where lovers had crawled in like badgers except that badgers didn't leave french-letters behind them, scattered like petals on trampled grass. He told her he'd be in touch. He told her how the poet went home: running like a horse at the last hills.

Dressing, stepping into his pants, he said: This teacher we had long ago, Gordon called him Crippen.

—Gordon, Gordon, Gordon.

—He was a good and proper man and religious. If he went to a dress dance he went first to the church and did the Stations of the Cross. You wouldn't know what they were.

—But my head was in the skies and the glory of God was upon me: and man or woman I should have bothered you as long as your noses were in the mud. Ladvenu, have you forgotten who I am?

She poured him strong black coffee.

—And it was a strange sight on a summer evening to see a man in full regimentals, white shirt, bow-tie, claw-hammer coat, following Christ, Simon the Cyrenean, along the Way of the Cross. He was a good man. He never married.

—No wonder.

—He had more to think of. There was a girl in this town, she's a woman now, who said he would be the handsomest man in the town if he would only let his trousers down.

Then he told her about Dorrie and Madge and Gordon and the fountain-pen.

—Gordon, Gordon, Gordon was all she said.

Beyond the ridge of the Quarries there had been, might still be if the growing town had not eaten it up, a pre-Celtic sun-circle of stones. The local people, for no sensible or scholarly reason, called it: The Giant's Grave. Crippen, who is now dead, used to walk his class out to study those stones and, since he was easy-going and innocent and never let his trousers down, half the class would vanish on the way. She said she would call to see Sadie before she followed on to the funeral. He crosses a red metal bridge. The river is high and breathing out mist. Even if there was a river-walk it would be thrice invisible: mist, half-darkness, brown flood-water. Wince, twice, thrice, frice, fice, sice, and seven-up. Repeat. He measures his steps in sevens and remembers joy. He turns a corner and walks on past the long wall of the military barracks. He is in another suburbia, tall old houses as yet undisturbed and unsurrounded. The road rises before him. Later when the town is awake it would be a good idea to pay Sadie a visit: lonely now with the two daft brothers dead. He runs like a horse at the last hill.

He kisses his sister. A cold lifeless kiss. Anyway northern people, apart from lovers and lechers, don't go in much for kissing when they meet and part. Once in happier days coming home, not drunk but merry, he had lifted his mother off the ground, hands under armpits, and danced and whirled her round and kissed her severeal, repeat severeal, times on both cheeks and, although she blushed and protested, he knew that she was delighted. It is not so with his sister. He feels that she shudders. She is tall and dark and with a stern strong profile. She has found him alone in the cold kitchen by a black dead range, his overcoat still on, a glass of whiskey in his hand, the bottle open on the range, Joan's Christmas cake on the table, it is sleeting outside. She is as cold as the kitchen. *Elle a raison, peut-être.* This is not the best way to come home for Christmas. She wears a blue woollen dressing-gown. She tells him that he is late. Or is it early? She waits to be informed. He says that things happened.

—They always do. You haven't favoured us with a visit in a long time. We were surprised when we heard from you. And now you come home like this. But I suppose you did come.

—I suppose I did.

—To meet old friends.

—And make new ones. Make new friends but keep the old: those are silver, these are gold.

—You were always good in company. Better than at home. I suppose you'll want breakfast. Or are you having it?

She brews tea. She tells him that Gordon was asking for him. Gordon, Gordon, Gordon.

—He was wondering if ever again you'd come home to see us.

—I came.

—You came all right. You're there for all to see. Or only poor me.

—I'll see Gordon tomorrow.

—I daresay you will.

He sips whiskey, looks out at sleet. She goes here and there, rattles cutlery. She says: How is her ladyship?

—Well. I hear. She acknowledges the alimony.

—The separation allowance. And the children.

—Well, too. I see them regularly.

—It's a pity you can't bring them home with you.

—Pity? Is it? Pity, pity. Oh, the pity of it.

—The town would talk.

—So you said. About where is she, where'er she be, the quite impossible she. The town's quiet this morning. For the birth of Christ. Let he who is without sin. And a rock came through the air and clobbered the woman. And Christ said: Oh mother.

—That's a way to talk on a Christmas morning. Are you drunk already?

He may be. Wince, twice, thrice. Bread has no sorrow for me. She sits across from him and sips tea. The house is a tomb above them. His mother sleeps. He says: To communicate. The need, the desire to communicate.

A clock strikes nine.

—What, she asks him, would you have to communicate?

He doesn't tell her but he thinks: a lot, a lot, a boy in a bath-chair, memories of joy, present sorrow, evil greyhounds in cages, a singing man who is never going back to Portadown, an Ulster detective who speaks Connacht Irish, a naked smiling girl with a glass middle, the queen riding straddle above the plains of delight, a horse of a poet running the hills home, a German child falling into shallow water, and all the world and dreams and dreams and dreams.

So as soon as it is decent, and the sleet ended, he walks across the town to see Sadie. He speaks to few people in the awakening streets. Mostly, he is happy to see, they're past and gone before they recognize him. He senses that. He walks fast. He doesn't look back. Were you ever out in the Great Alone? Read that out, young Lisney, and prove that your father isn't wasting his money sending you to school. But the kitchen that was once all light, warmth, company, bottled stout, poetry, poker-schools is now a store-room stuffed with cardboard boxes, the shop is shut for ever, she shows him around, she lives upstairs and lets the ground floor to a man in stationery and light hardware, wholesale. Have you whistled bits of ragtime at the end of all creation and learned to know the desert's little ways. The man should have written: Dusty face. Another man did.

—How was it at home, Jim Lisney?

—Cold, cold. *Sé tá, fuar, fuar.* My mother cried to see me.

—Mothers cry. At least you had a Christmas cake for her.

—She was here so?

—She was.

—And gone?

—And gone. She said to tell you that bread had no sorrow for her and water no affliction. She said to tell you she'd gone to the fire. Like yourself she's not so good at the homecoming or at staying when she gets there. That was what her mother said to me when I went a week to London——

—The sights of Soho. The noblest prospect a likely girl can behold.

—To ask Tilly to come home to see them, and I did, where she works in a shop, typewriters and record-players and things, in Kensington. Your mother says come home and see them. She said, My mother's not my mother.

—Her mother's not her mother. She's Joan the Boy. She's Tilly. She's a boy in a wheelchair. A woman in a bed.

—Did you treat her well?

—To the best of my ability.

—No cheap jokes.

—Sadie, I don't feel like joking.

She stands on her tiptoes and scans him. For Christmas morning the kohl has been removed: No, I don't think you do. As I say, you weren't the worst. How under God did you come to make such a mess of your life? Look at Gordon. The wildest of all of you. Settled.

Gordon, Gordon, Gordon, Sir Gordon, Skinny, Nero, Ladvenu.

—But Sadie, he married an Englishwoman. Direct rule was imposed.

Then: Her mother is not her mother. You said, she said.

—She didn't tell you? Well it's her own business, not yours or mine, and then she said to me, walking in Kensington Gardens: I'll be home for my grandmother's funeral. And I said she isn't dead and she said again: I'll be home for my grandmother's funeral.

—But her grandmother is dead.

—Of course she is. Joan's gone on to the funeral.

—She's gone.

—I told you already. She said to tell you she had gone to the fire. Ten minutes ago in a taxi. But her grandmother wasn't dead when we were walking in Kensington Gardens and she said, and don't tell a soul Jim Lisney, two evenings ago, she said, I saw her standing under that tree.

—Under a tree.

—In Kensington Gardens.

The bells are ringing wild: Come all to church good people. Sadie is dressed to go to Mass. Demure, black coat, black hat and veil, mourning two daft or part-time daft brothers. Far away one of them plays Tarzan on a sunny river-bank and the nurses laugh from the bridge knowing that they'll get him in the end: part-time anyway. Have you swept the visioned valley with the green stream streaking through it?

—The bells are ringing, Jim Lisney. You could come to Mass with me. *Adeste fideles.*

—Her grandmother, you mean, died after that, after Kensington?

—You often find that, Jim, a fierce closeness between grandparents and grandchildren, something we can't see jumps a generation, like green fingers or a taste for music or a sweet tooth, more so in her case, closer than twins, it saved her when they told her, you'll want to know, now I've said so much, when she was fourteen they told her, stupid to bother but somebody else might have told her, that her mother wasn't her mother, her father was her father, if you know what I mean, the grandmother was the father's mother.

—I can guess.

—You've a great brain, Jim Lisney, my brothers always said you were the cleverest boy ever read out loud in the kitchen behind the shop. But. The news distracted her. She was in a home for a bit. Like my brothers. She kept saying she was two people. The granny came and saved her.

—The granny's dead now. Under a tree in Kensington Gardens. Peter Pan and all. But to shut me from the light of the sky and the sight of the fields and flowers.

On the sunny riverbank Tarzan knew he was twenty people.

—Jim Lisney, you're rambling. The bells have stopped. We'll be late walking up the aisle. But, even at that, it would please your mother and sister to see you at Mass.

She takes his arm, the key of the door in her other hand, he carries her handbag.

—I'll look inside for the last time. This room may be gone when I'm here again.

They stand in the doorway. The cardboard boxes have smothered even the range on which so many glasses and black bottles had rested and made rings. He says: I'll say them a poem. They'll hear me wherever they are.

—Jim Lisney, you're crazy. But you're good. They'll hear you.

She is crying. Very quietly.

He stands in the centre of the floor and reaches out his right hand as if he were holding a book and goes, as bold as Demosthenes, into his act: A bunch of the boys were whooping it up in the Malemute Saloon.